*"Sore losers are not welcome
in this game."*

"I ain't leaving while all of my money is on the table in front of you, Adams."

"You've got enough in front of you for a meal and a hotel room somewhere," Clint said slowly, "but not in this town, Farmer. Get up and walk out."

"You walk out, and leave the money on the table—or else they'll carry you out."

Clint sighed. He still had the deck of cards in his left hand.

"The amount of money you've lost here isn't worth dying for, Farmer, believe me. Why don't we just wait for the sheriff—"

"I ain't waitin'," Farmer said, shoving back from the table . . .

Don't miss any of the lusty, hard-riding action in the Charter Western series, THE GUNSMITH

And coming next month:
THE GUNSMITH #69: TRAIL DRIVE TO MONTANA

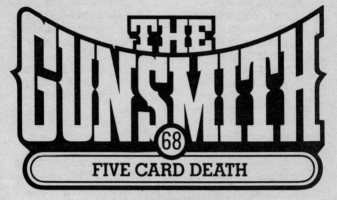

THE GUNSMITH

68

FIVE CARD DEATH

J. R. ROBERTS

JOVE BOOKS, NEW YORK

THE GUNSMITH #68: FIVE CARD DEATH

A Jove Book / published by arrangement with
the author

PRINTING HISTORY
Jove edition / August 1987

ISBN: 0-515-09118-9

Jove Books are published by The Berkley Publishing Group,
200 Madison Avenue, New York, New York 10016.
The name "JOVE" and the "J" logo
are trademarks belonging to Jove Publications, Inc.

PRINTED IN THE UNITED STATES OF AMERICA

10 9 8 7 6 5 4 3 2 1

PROLOGUE
Jericho Flats, Colorado

Clint Adams did not need to check his cards. He had seen them once already, and once was enough. He had a ten of diamonds and an eight of diamonds on the table, along with a nine of clubs and a six of hearts. Not showing was a queen of diamonds and a jack of diamonds. In other words, he already had a straight, but with one more card coming he needed another diamond for a flush—and a nine of diamonds for a straight flush.

Well, he figured, that's worth a raise.

"I raise a hundred," he said.

The other players around the table alternately checked their cards or simply stared at him.

The Jericho Flats poker game had been inaugurated ten years ago, and had been held every six months ever since. It usually lasted two or three days, with short intermissions. Sleeping was something that was put off for another time. There were ten players invited, but rarely did more than six show up at one time. There were usually only that many within riding distance when January 15 and July 15 came around.

Clint himself had attended the game six times in the past ten years.

The other players at this game were:

Jock Reynolds, the town blacksmith, who not many people knew had more money than a normal

1

blacksmith. The people who did know didn't ask where it came from, as long as he dropped some of it at the game. He lived in Jericho Flats, and he was the host of the game. He was a man in his fifties with big beefy shoulders and a crop of salt-and-pepper hair that got more salt and less pepper with each year.

Dan Arcel, whose only love in life was gambling. He had been at the game five times that Clint knew of. He was a small, dapper man whose hands were so fast he probably could have cheated if he wanted to, but he never did. Clint enjoyed playing him. He considered him the best player of the group.

Sam Jennings, a banker from the nearby town of Waterhole, which had one right in the middle of Main Street!

Al Collins, a newspaperman who was always on the go, but usually managed to attend the game once a year.

Ed Ransom, a traveling salesman. Clint suspected that he didn't play with his own money, and wondered what he told his employers when he lost.

The players who were not present this time were:

Luke Short, the legendary gambler and gunman.

Bat Masterson, also known for his gambling and gunwork. Bat was a close friend of Clint's, while Luke Short was simply a friend. There was a difference.

Talbot Roper, a private detective who once worked for Pinkerton until old Allan and he agreed that he didn't fit the Pinkerton mold. Tal had his own agency now, in Denver.

The tenth player was Joe Kelly, and he wasn't present because he was dead—but that subject didn't come up until after the game was over.

As Clint had hoped, everyone saw his raise and stayed in for the last card. The only one he was worried about was Arcel. He only stayed when he had something or he was going to run a huge bluff. Clint didn't think he was bluffing this time. The others were not professional cardplayers, and often stayed for the last card—and a prayer.

"Deal," Clint said to Jock, and the man's huge hands doled out six last cards.

Clint looked at his once, and then left it on the table.

"Aces bet," Jock said to Sam Jennings.

"I look like that much of a fool?" Jennings asked. "I'll check to the raiser."

"Same here," Collins said.

Ransom nodded, and Jock said, "I fold." Clint was glad to see that. Jock had lost heavily this time. "The bet's to you, Clint."

"I bet a hundred."

He tossed the money into the pot, where it landed soundlessly. They didn't bother with chips in this game. They used paper money.

The bet was now up to Arcel, who had a pair of deuces sitting on the table, and not much else. Clint had not seen any other twos on the table, however, and it was quite possible that Arcel had four of them, or maybe three to a full house. He had *something* or he wouldn't be here.

And he wouldn't be raising.

"I see your hundred and raise five."

A murmur went up from around the table and one by one the other players dropped out.

"This looks like the last hand of the game, Dan," Clint said, "so let's make it interesting. I'll see your five hundred and raise five."

"You call that interesting?" Arcel asked, grinning.

"Well, it's civilized interesting," Clint said. He'd played in bigger games before, but found that he didn't enjoy it as much. He hoped that Arcel wouldn't raise the ante much more.

"All right," Arcel said, "civilized interesting. I call your five hundred."

Clint turned over his hole cards, showing everyone the diamonds—including the nine for the straight flush.

"Son of a bitch!" Arcel said without rancor. He turned over his hole cards to reveal two more deuces.

"Four deuces!" Sam Jennings said, shaking his head.

"Straight flush takes it," Jock Reynolds said, "and that does it, gentlemen. Time for food and drink."

Everyone gathered their money off the table and started for the long wooden table that had been set up at the other end of the livery by Jock's young daughter, Mickey, whose real name was Michelle. She had done the cooking, and the spread included chicken, corn on the cob, baked potatoes, and fresh biscuits.

Clint and Arcel were the last to leave the table, since they had the most money to put away.

"Heard from Luke or Bat lately, Clint?" Arcel asked. There was no point in discussing the hand. It was over.

"Bat's in Dodge last I heard. Lost track of Luke, but he's someplace with a deck of cards in his hands, that's for sure."

"What about Roper?"

"Working," Clint said, and offered no further explanation. "What do you hear from Joe Kelly?"

"You haven't heard?"

"Heard what?"

"Kelly's dead."

"What?"

Kelly was a Federal marshal, but he never wore his badge when he came to the game.

"What happened?"

"Somebody got the drop on him in a hotel room in Columbus."

"Ohio? Or New Mexico?"

"New Mexico."

"Who could get the drop on Joe?"

Arcel shrugged.

"It was done, and that's that. Shot him and got away clean."

"When was this?"

"Last month. It was in some of the papers."

"I missed it. Damn! Joe Kelly."

"Yeah. Come on, let's go and eat."

"Do the others know?"

Arcel shrugged.

"If they ask we'll tell them, but why bring it up?"

"I guess you're right. It'll come up, though. One of us getting killed, that's got to affect the others."

"Yeah," Arcel said, "now we'll have to replace him in the game."

Clint was curious about Joe Kelly's death, so when he left Jericho Flats on his way back to Labyrinth, Texas, he decided to swing by Columbus, New Mexico, to ask a few questions.

Columbus was just barely in New Mexico, sitting in the southeast corner just two or three miles from the Texas border, so it wasn't that much of a detour for Clint on the way to Labyrinth.

When he rode into Columbus he left Duke at the livery with instructions to care for him, but to have him ready to leave. Clint did not intend to stay the night.

He went to the sheriff's office and introduced himself. As with most lawmen—especially those in their late thirties to middle forties—he was recognized and welcomed.

"Be glad to help you in any way I can, Mr.

Adams,'' Sheriff Horace Taylor said. Taylor was on the far side of forty, a sleepy-looking man who had been sheriff in Columbus for more than ten years. This led Clint to believe that the sleepy look was deceiving.

"I'm interested in what happened to Marshal Joe Kelly here last month, Sheriff."

"Terrible thing, him having such a reputation and all. Didn't rightly know what to do about it."

"How's that?"

"Well, where he was found, I mean. After all, he was married, wasn't he?"

"He was," Clint said, although he knew that the Kelly marriage was not much of one. Joe was on the road most of the time, and Lily had pretty well accepted that and made a life for herself without him back East somewhere. According to Joe, the separation had been amiable, and he went to visit her on occasion.

"Where was he found, Sheriff?"

"Over in the whorehouse, naked as you please in one of the rooms."

"Was he a customer?"

"That's just the thing," Taylor said, shaking his head. "Ol' Tessie, the madam, she said she never saw him before she heard the shot, rushed up and found him there, dead in one of her beds."

"Any of the girls admit to being with him?"

"Not a one, and I can't say I rightly blame them for that."

"No, I guess not. Would you mind if I talked to this Tessie?"

"Be my guest. Tell her I said it was okay."

"Thanks, Sheriff."

"And if you're thinking of sampling her stock," the lawman said with a wink, "tell her to give you

Mildred. Girl ain't much to look at, but she's hell-on-wheels in bed.''

"I'll keep that in mind, Sheriff. Thanks."

Riding out of Columbus just hours after riding in, Clint reflected back on what he'd found out.

Madam Tessie's story had been just as the sheriff had related it. She'd never seen Joe Kelly before finding him dead in one of her beds.

Clint had questioned several of her girls, but none of them admitted to Clint that they had been with Kelly. (The sheriff had been right about Mildred not being one to look at, but Clint would take the lawman's word for the rest.)

Now, as Clint rode out, he wondered what Joe Kelly had done to get himself killed, and who he had done it to. If it had been a simple case of a grudge, or of a young gun trying to make a rep off an old—or older—one, then it would have happened in the street or, as in the case of Hickok, in a saloon. This, however, was a little weird. Someone had apparently knocked him out, dragged him up to the room in the whorehouse—*without being seen*—and then shot him and escaped—again, without being seen.

Why would someone go through all that trouble?

Outside of town Clint changed his direction and rode toward Texas, wondering if he would be leaving so readily if he and Joe Kelly had been very close friends instead of acquaintances and occasional poker buddies.

If it had been Bat Masterson who had been killed—or even Luke Short, for that matter—he'd be sticking around to ask some more questions. If he and Kelly had been better friends he'd be talking to the man's boss, and maybe even to Kelly's wife, back East.

As it stood now, though, a man he knew had been killed under odd circumstances. He was sorry, and he had been curious enough to stop off for a few hours in the town where it had happened. He wasn't, however, prepared to launch a time-consuming investigation into the man's death.

As he had told people many times before, he wasn't a damn detective . . .

ONE

A month later Clint was sitting in Rick Hartman's saloon with Rick himself. It was early and the place was empty. Rick's girls were all upstairs asleep, since their working hours didn't start until the sun was on the way down.

T.C., the bartender, a big man with large biceps, came over and poured them each another cup of coffee.

"Thanks, T.C.," Rick said.

Clint picked up the cup and sipped it. Ambrosia. Black and strong, just the way he liked it. Clint knew very little about the bartender, but he knew that the man made the best coffee he'd ever tasted.

"That man is a treasure."

"Don't let him hear you," Rick said. "He'll demand a raise."

Clint was laughing when he saw the batwing doors open. He always sat facing the doors, something he'd learned from Wild Bill Hickok—or rather, from the way Wild Bill Hickok died.

"Mickey?" he said, staring in disbelief.

Rick turned and watched as the short, pretty but disheveled-looking girl walked over to the table.

"Hi, Clint."

"What are you doing here?" Clint asked. "Is your pa with you?"

She shook her head. Her brown hair was cut short,

and her clothes were dirty and too big for her. It was only the fact that she *was* so pretty that kept her from being mistaken for a boy—a fourteen-year-old boy.

"My pa's not here, Clint, but he's the one who sent me to see you."

"Are you going to introduce us?" Rick asked.

"Sure. Rick Hartman, meet Michelle Reynolds —only Michelle would rather be called Mickey."

"Why? Michelle is such a pretty name," Rick said.

"Pa wanted a boy," Mickey said candidly. "Clint, can we talk?"

"You can sit right here and tell me what's on your mind. Are you hungry?"

"I could use something to eat, I guess. I rode most of the night."

"I'll get her something," Rick said, standing up. "How do you like your eggs, Michelle?"

"Sunny side up, I guess."

"You have your talk with Clint and I'll get you some breakfast."

It was almost lunchtime, but that didn't matter. To Clint Mickey looked hungry enough to eat anything that was put in front of her.

And she looked worried.

"What's wrong, Mickey?"

"Somebody wants to kill you, Clint."

"Kill me? You rode all this way to tell me that?"

"To warn you."

"What makes you think that somebody wants to kill me?"

"Pa says."

"And what makes him think it's true?"

"Joe Kelly's dead."

"I know that—"

"And Sam Jennings, and Al Collins, too."

"What?"

"Somebody shot them."

"Jesus. I didn't hear."

"Pa heard. He says somebody is killing the people who play in his poker game. He wants you to warn everyone, because they'll listen to you."

"Your pa may have a point," Clint said. He was a firm disbeliever in coincidence, and for three men to be killed—three men who played in the same poker game—well, that was too much for him to swallow.

"Has your pa been in contact with the others?"

She shook her head.

"He wanted me to tell you to contact them. He figures men like Roper, Short, and Masterson would take it more serious if they heard it from you."

"And Arcel and Ransom?"

"He couldn't find them."

That made sense. Arcel was a gambler, and Ransom a salesmen, and they both traveled a lot.

"I'll have to see if I can locate them."

T.C. came over with a glass of milk for Mickey and more coffee for Clint.

"Breakfast is almost ready, little lady. The boss is making it himself."

"Thank you," she said. The glass of milk was huge, but she downed half of it very quickly.

Clint Adams knew that Jock Reynolds was no fool. He could have notified Clint by telegram, but he'd sent his daughter here to get her out of harm's way. He obviously felt that she was safer with Clint than she would be with her father, even though if someone *was* killing players in their game, they were both in danger.

"Mr. Adams?"

"Yes, Mickey."

"I'm real worried about my pa."

"I don't blame you, Mickey, but don't worry too much. I'll be leaving for Jericho Flats in the morning. Your pa's not going to be alone."

"Good. I'll be ready to leave—"

"No, I think it's best you stay here, Mickey."

"Why?"

"Because your father and I are going to have to worry about ourselves. If we have to worry about you, too, one or both of us could end up dead, and we don't want that, do we?"

She set her jaw stubbornly and didn't answer. At that point Rick came out with her breakfast and she unset her jaw to eat it. Clint stood up and walked off with Rick.

"What'd you say to her to get her so mad?"

"I told her I want her to stay here," Clint said. Very quickly he explained the situation to Rick.

"As bad as it looks, Clint, it could be coincidence."

"Could be, but I'm not buying it. I want her to be safe, Rick, even if her pa and I are barking up the wrong tree."

"All right. I'll let the girls take care of her."

"Good, just do me one favor, okay?"

"Sure."

"Don't go making a saloon girl out of her."

Rick grinned and said, "That's me, get-em-while-they're-young Hartman."

TWO

Clint asked Hartman to do something else for him.

"What?"

"Use your grapevine to find out where Dan Arcel and a man named Ed Ransom are."

"Arcel I've heard of. He's a gambler."

"Right."

"Who's Ransom."

"He's a salesman."

"Why not contact his company and find out where he is? They should know."

"That would be a good idea, except that I don't know who his company is. In fact, I don't even know what he sells."

"You been playing poker with the man for ten years and you don't know what he sells?"

"Four years. Ransom joined the game four years ago, and no, all we care about is that he shows up with money."

"How many original players are still in the game?" Rick asked.

"There's Jock, who started it, me, Arcel, Luke Short, Bat and Tal Roper."

"All the others have been replacements over the years?"

"That's right."

"Well, there you have another one."

"Another what?"

"Connection or coincidence, whatever you want to call it. All of the dead players have been replacements. Maybe the originals aren't in danger."

"If that's true then Ransom is still in danger. I'm not going to assume that, Rick. I'm going to notify Luke, Bat, and Tal about what's happened. Meanwhile, you try and locate the other two. I'd like to get to them before I reach Jericho Flats."

"All right. Let me wake Lily and tell her to watch over the girl. When the other girls wake up they'll take turns keeping her entertained."

Lily was Rick's current favorite among his girls. He only hired the finest, lovliest women, and for that reason usually chose among them for his own bed partners.

Of this current batch Clint's favorite was a dark-haired girl named Roxanne, who was not asleep in her room like the other girls, but asleep in *his* bed in *his* hotel room.

"Want to put her in the hotel?" Rick asked, indicating Mickey.

"Have you got a room here?"

"Sure."

"Then keep her here. She'll be safer."

"All right. She's almost finished eating, so let me get Lily and then I'll send some wires."

"Okay. Thanks, Rick."

"Sure."

Clint walked back to the table where Mickey was finishing her meal and sat with her.

"Mickey, I'm going to introduce you to a lady named Lily. She's going to be your very best friend until this is all over with."

"I don't need a best friend," Mickey said sullenly. "I need my pa."

"Since your pa sent you to me for safekeeping, young lady, you'll do as I say." Not having any children of his own, Clint was unsure as to how to handle Mickey, but he'd decided to simply flex his muscles and see what happened.

Apparently it had worked, for Mickey looked down at the top of the table and said, "Yes, sir."

Rick came down the steps and walked over to the table. Behind him a lovely, sleepy woman with blond hair came down, wearing a lavender dressing gown. Even with her face puffed from sleep you could see what a beauty she was. She was much more beautiful than Roxanne, but then there were other things about Roxanne that Clint liked. He rarely picked a woman for her looks alone.

"Mickey, this is Lily."

"Hi, honey," Lily said, crouching down next to the fourteen-year-old girl.

Mickey looked at Lily and her eyes widened.

"You're beautiful!" she said in awe.

Lily smiled at the compliment and became even more beautiful.

"Thank you. You're very pretty yourself."

"No, I ain't."

"Yes, you are, and I can prove it, too."

"How?"

"You come with me," Lily said. She stood up and took Mickey by the shoulders, lifting her off her chair to her feet. "We're going to get you a bath, and then I'm going to show you a Michelle you've never seen before."

"My name's Mickey."

"After I'm through with you," Lily said, winking at Rick, "your name will be Michelle, and you'll never want to be Mickey again." Lily looked over her shoulder at Clint and Rick and said, "Don't you men have things to do?"

"We sure do," Rick said.

"Then go do them. Michelle and I are going to get

along just fine. Come on, honey."

Meekly, Mickey–Michelle allowed herself to be steered to the steps and started up, with Lily behind her, talking to her urgently.

"Lily's got a way with people," Rick said admiringly.

"Men people, or kid people?" Clint asked.

"All people."

"You might be right, Rick," Clint said, but Mickey had gone along with Lily just a little *too* easily for his taste. If she had any of her father's stubbornness in her, she was planning something.

Clint was not looking forward to finding out what it was.

THREE

Clint's favorite thing about Roxanne Dubois was her hair. It was as black as the inside of a mine shaft when there's absolutely no light coming from anywhere. It was long, hanging all the way to her shapely butt in shimmering waves, and he loved to watch her sit and brush it, as she did before bed each night.

Not as classically beautiful as Rick's Lily, Roxanne had a face made of seemingly mismatching parts. Her eyes were widely set, brown and large, her eyebrows very dark. She refused to "shape" her eyebrows as some women did, plucking hairs out to make them arch this way or that. Clint loved her eyebrows. He thought they did a lot for her face, which was angular, with high cheekbones and a long chin. Her mouth was wide, but while the lower lip was full and lush, the upper was slim and sort of curled in a funny way when she talked. When she smiled it was more to one side of her mouth than the other, giving her face a slightly lopsided look. Her nose was long, with large nostrils that flared during sex.

Her eyes, eyebrows, nose, cheekbones, mouth, all the parts that made up her face seemed to have been taken from other faces and thrown together here. And as mismatched as they appeared to be, when you put them altogether you got a face so arresting that Clint had looked at it even before Lily's beautiful one.

When Clint went back to his room to wake her so that she could help with Mickey, he found that she was already awake. When he walked in she sat up and stretched, causing the sheet to fall away from the upper portion of her body. He stood and admired her breasts. They were long and set rather widely apart, so that there was a definite valley between them, and not just the cleavage of larger busted girls, whose breasts touched. Her nipples were very brown with large, almost perfectly round aureoles. He couldn't see it now but he had firsthand experience with the tangle of thick black hair between her legs, which he referred to as "her furry little beast." Many times had his penis been swallowed by that furry little beast, but it never seemed to be enough times.

Standing there now, just watching her, he felt himself begin to swell.

"Good morning," she said, dropping her hands down into her lap.

"Morning? More like afternoon?"

"Is it late?"

"Not for afternoon it's not," he said, approaching the bed. "Come on, lazy, get up. I've got a favor I'd like you to do for me."

"Um-hmm, and I've got a favor I'd like you to do for me," she said, reaching up for his arm and pulling him down beside her.

"What's that?"

She smiled and leaned forward so she could use her tongue to outline his mouth. He felt his thickening penis twitch as she did this.

With her mouth right up against his she answered in a whisper, "Feed the beast."

How could he refuse a plea like that?

Roxanne was tall, even lying down.

As they lay side by, face to face, her feet almost

reached his. They kissed, tasting and nipping, while their hands roamed about, touching, feeling, stroking, all in preamble to what would come later. They had both found that they liked working up to it with each other; they enjoyed the little touches and kisses almost as much as the final act.

Clint particularly enjoyed running his hands through Roxanne's long black tresses, and she, for some reason, enjoying rubbing her palms over his lean flanks.

When her hand snaked between them to grasp his rigid penis, it was her signal that she was ready for some serious lovemaking. Sometimes it was he who gave the signal, but in any case they got to it pretty quickly.

The kisses deepened, and his hands moved between them so that his fingers could feel her moistness, probing and rubbing, until she was panting against his mouth.

He moved down then so that his mouth could work on her, his tongue sliding up and down the slick lips of her vagina, delving inside fleetingly, teasingly. He slid his hands beneath her buttocks, gripping her tightly and lifting her to him as he finally thrust his tongue all the way in, then out, and then around her turgid clit, teasing her even more, building her toward a shattering climax. She moaned and writhed on the bed and lifted her hips herself so that it was no longer necessary for him to bear her weight.

When she came she made a high, keening sound and he quickly moved up and over her and slid into her while she was still riding the waves of pleasure from the first orgasm. He drove himself deeply into her and she reached around to grab his buttocks as she experienced a second climax.

"Now . . ." she said breathlessly. "Clint . . . now . . . you . . ."

He moved in and out of her in long, even strokes, gently at first and then with increasing speed until finally they were lunging at each other, striving for that final explosion that would leave them both spent and satiated until next time . . .

"You want me to baby sit a fourteen-year-old?" Roxanne asked in disbelief.

"Her father is a friend of mine, and he's in some danger. He sent her to me to protect her."

"So then why do I—"

"I'm leaving town to go and see her father. He needs my protection more than she does."

"So she's agreed to stay here with me and Lily and the other girls?"

"I badgered her into it."

"You think so, huh?"

"Why not?"

She ran her hand over his chest and said, "I'm just remembering what I was like at fourteen."

"Beautiful, no doubt."

"That's another story, but I was thinking more of how stubborn I was. I never let any adult badger me into anything I didn't want to do."

"You think this girl is the same way?"

"I don't know, Clint, I haven't met her. What do you think?"

"I did think that she gave in a little too easily," Clint admitted.

"I'll talk to Lily and see what she thinks, and then I'll talk to—what's her name, Michelle?"

"She prefers Mickey."

"We can fix that easily enough, but I'll talk to her and see what I think."

Clint sat up in bed.

"Where are you going?"

"I've got some things I've got to do to get ready to

leave, and I've allowed you to distract me long enough.''

"Is that what I am, a distraction?''

He glanced at her to see how serious her question was, and there was enough humor on her face to tell him that she was only half serious.

"A distraction, a diversion, whatever word you want to put to it, but whatever it is you do it so well.''

"That's a compliment—I think.''

"Come on,'' he said, slapping her on the rump, "get up and dressed and let's get moving. We've both got some work to do so that I can get started in the morning.''

"Baby sitter,'' Roxanne said, shaking her head as she rose from the bed. "Me! That is certainly not what I anticipated when I came to this town.''

"I'll make it up to you.''

"When?''

"When I get back.''

"And when will that be?''

Dressed by now, he kissed her on the nose and said, "As soon as I can. I'll see you over at the saloon later.''

"All right.''

As Clint Adams left, Roxanne mulled his answer to her last question.

He'd be back as soon as he could.

She knew enough about Clint Adams as the Gunsmith to know that there was another answer to that.

He'd be back *if* he could—if he was still alive.

FOUR

After Clint left Roxanne he went to the telegraph office. He drafted three telegrams that were roughly the same and sent them out. One went to Denver, to Talbot Roper's office. The other one went to Dodge City, where Bat Masterson might or might not have still been. The third he sent to several different towns that were known for their gambling—Tombstone, Leadville, even San Francisco—hoping to catch Luke Short at one of them. The three telegrams warned them and mentioned the deaths of Kelly, Jennings, and Collins.

These men were all experienced, and could all draw their own conclusions and act accordingly. Clint added one extra line telling them that he was on his way to Jericho Flats, and they could contact him there. Hopefully, the fact that he was going would keep *them* from going. They would all make harder targets if there were hundreds of miles between them, and not all of them congregated in the same town.

After that, Clint went to the livery to tell the liveryman to have Duke ready in the morning, and he went to the general store to pick up some supplies for his ride to Jericho Flats.

Finally, he managed to get back to the saloon, where Rick was waiting.

"Find out anything?"

"I haven't located Ransom, but I found Arcel."

"Where is he?"

"Texas."

"You're kidding?"

"Up around Amarillo."

The panhandle, Clint thought.

"That's great. Can we get him a telegram?"

"I said he was around Amarillo. I can send a telegram there, but there's no telling if he'll get it or not."

"Give it a try. I'll head that way and see if I can catch up with him. Where's Mickey."

"Upstairs with Lily and Roxanne. They're making her look like more of a Michelle than a Mickey."

"What do you think, Rick? Will she sit still after I'm gone?"

"You'll have to ask the girls that, Clint. I haven't even spoken to her since breakfast, but she's been with Lily since then, and seemed to hit it right off with Roxanne. How are you and Roxanne getting along, by the way?"

"Fine. Why?"

"I'm just waiting for the day one of these women is going to reel you in, that's all."

"And what about you and Lily?"

"We're doing fine, but I'm a hard catch, even if I had the hook in my mouth—which I don't."

"Well, neither do I."

"I hope neither one of us ends up lying at the bottom of a dry lake, all by ourselves."

"I hope that's your last morbid thought of the day."

At that point Roxanne came downstairs and approached them.

"Where's Mickey?"

"Upstairs with Lily."

"Have you spoken with her?"

"And with Lily. We've both come to the same conclusion, Clint."

"What's that?"

"Once you leave town, this little girl is gonna be on your tail first chance she gets."

Clint looked at Rick, who shrugged.

"You'll have to sit on her," Clint told the both of them.

"What do you expect us to do, Clint?" Rick asked. "Keep her prisoner?"

"She's got every right to go home, you know," Roxanne added.

"Are you all on her side? The girl could end up getting hurt, you know."

"If her father gets killed while she's here, that's going to hurt a lot more," Roxanne said.

Clint opened his mouth to reply, then shut it, realizing that he had none.

"What makes you so smart?"

"God gave me looks *and* brains," she bragged, "while he only gave you one."

As she turned and trotted up the stairs he shouted out, "Yeah, but which one?"

He looked at Rick, who shrugged again.

"Don't look at me. I didn't think you had either in any great abundance."

"My friend."

Clint left the saloon to finalize preparations for his leaving the following morning. He wondered if he shouldn't just plan to take Mickey along with him if there was a chance that she was going to follow him anyway.

He checked with the telegraph office to see if there were any replies to his telegrams. There was one from Dodge City from someone named Hansen who said that Bat Masterson was not in town just then, but that Hansen would get the message to him as soon as possible.

There was one from Denver saying that Talbot Roper was away on a case, and that his exact whereabouts were unknown at this time.

There were no replies from any of the towns Clint had sent telegrams to in an attempt to find Luke Short.

It was discouraging that he had not been able to contact any of his friends and warn them that there might be an attempt on their lives. Still, all three of them were well able to take care of themselves.

But then, he would have thought the same thing about Joe Kelly.

He went back to the saloon that night when it was packed and asked Roxanne, who was working, where Mickey was.

"This is no place for her when we're busy," Roxanne said, "so I left her up in my room."

"Doing what?"

Roxanne shrugged.

"Whatever a fourteen-year-old girl does when she's in a room alone."

Clint frowned and hurried upstairs. He knocked on the door of Roxanne's room and when there was no answer he opened it, knowing what he would find.

Nothing.

"What's wrong?" Roxanne asked, coming up from behind him.

"She's gone."

"What do you mean, gone?"

"I mean she didn't wait for me to leave so she could follow me," Clint said. "She's started ahead of me."

"Oh," Roxanne said, putting her hands over her mouth. "I'm sorry—"

"Never mind," Clint said, taking her by the shoulders. "What did you and others tell her?"

"What do you—"

"Did anyone tell her that I was heading for Amarillo to find Arcel?"

She frowning, concentrating, and then said, "I'm sure one of us told her. I think it was Lily, but I'm sure she didn't mean any—"

"I'm not going to scold her," Clint said. "At least if she's going to Amarillo I can catch up to her and still find Dan Arcel."

"Where are you going?" she called out as he rushed past her from the room.

"If I'm going to catch her I've got to start tonight."

Roxanne rushed out into the hall and called out, "Isn't it dangerous to ride at night?"

"That's why I've got to leave now and find her," Clint called back over his shoulder. "Now!"

FIVE

Clint caught up to her much quicker than he thought he would.

Well, actually, the fact that she had camped and was waiting for him helped a lot.

He had been riding an hour when he saw the light from her fire. He didn't know it was her fire, of course, until he got closer and saw her, hunched over the flames, warming her hands.

When he walked into the camp, leading Duke, she looked up and said, "Well, it's about time. I thought I was going to starve."

Clint made coffee and beans from his stores and passed her a plate.

"You were pretty damn sure I'd come after you tonight, weren't you?"

"Yes."

"Why?"

"Because my pa always says that you act fast. He says your reactions are the quickest he's ever seen, with or without a gun."

"And you were prepared to bet on that?"

"I won, didn't I?"

"That depends."

"On what?"

"On whether or not I decide to take you over my knee."

29

"You wouldn't!"

"Don't tempt me."

"I'm not a child. I did what my pa is always telling me to do."

"What's that?"

"He says that I should always do what I feel is right."

"And you felt that this was right? Riding out here in the dark alone?"

"I felt it was more right than staying in that town and letting those women turn me into something I'm not—or try."

"Those ladies happen to be very nice women."

"They're pretty, all right, and I guess they're nice, but I couldn't just stay behind and let them change me while you and my pa were in danger. I've got to get back to him, Mr. Adams. He needs me."

Clint regarded her for a long moment, and then said, "I'm sure he does need you, Mickey."

"Then you won't take me back to town?"

"I'd like to, but I don't want to take the time. We have to get up to Amarillo and see if we can find Dan Arcel. I'll also have to see if Rick has found out anything about Ed Ransom's whereabouts."

"Aren't we going to help my pa?"

"That's where we're headed, Mickey, but if we can stop along the way and warn someone else, don't you think we should? It might save their lives, too."

"I suppose so."

"Don't worry," he said. "We'll get to your pa and help him. He can take care of himself."

There was those words again. Kelly was more than able to take care of himself, and God knew, so was Wild Bill Hickok, but look what happened to them.

Luckily, Mickey seemed somewhat soothed by his words and started to eat her dinner.

Clint, less than mollified by his own words, hoped

that Jock Reynolds would be extra careful until they could join him in Jericho Flats. Between the two of them, maybe he and Jock could figure out who was behind this.

Clint checked the horses, tossed some more wood on the fire, and then lay down with his head on his saddle. He stared at the sliver of a moon in the sky and tried to figure out who would be killing the players in the Jericho Flats poker game.

As far as he knew, no player had ever been expelled from the game, so that meant that it wasn't some irate ex-player. The only ex-players were the dead players, or the players who had left of their own accord.

What did that leave? Not much. He couldn't think of any wild arguments that might have arisen during a game. Most of the players were fairly level-headed and businesslike in their play, and there were none who drank to excess during the game. He himself did not drink at all while playing. That was the easiest way to leave the game broke.

No, he couldn't think of one goddamned player who might have a grudge against the others, and that just didn't bode well for finding the killer.

SIX

They got an early start the next morning, and every morning after that. Their ride to Amarillo took the better part of a week, and Clint was surprised—though pleasantly so—that Mickey did not retard his progress at all. She kept up, and when a rest stop was necessary it was because her horse—a bay mare she called Lucky—could not keep up with Duke.

When they finally rode into Amarillo it was midday. They put the horses up at the livery and went to find the hotel.

Once Clint had taken two rooms for them, he took Mickey up to hers.

"I want you to stay here while I have a look around."

"Why can't I come with you?"

"Because I may have to go into a saloon or two, and I don't want to have you trailing behind me."

"I can look around, too."

"No good, Mickey."

"Why not?"

"Because if you're not with me, I want to know where you are and not have to wonder."

She was about to argue when she had to admit that what he said made sense.

"All right," she said, "I'll wait—but I'm hungry."

"So am I. After I've looked around some I'll come

back and we'll go and get some dinner."

"When will we be leaving?"

"With any luck, tomorrow. I'm hoping to find Arcel today, or at least to be able to leave him a message."

She rubbed her eyes and said, "Maybe I'll just close my eyes for a bit. It's been a while since I've been on a real bed. I'll see you shortly."

"All right."

As he headed for the door she sat on the bed, but as she was about to lie back she suddenly sat up again.

"Clint!"

"What?" he asked, turning to face her.

"Be careful."

"Don't worry. Get some sleep."

After Clint left the hotel he went directly to the saloon for a cold beer. As the bartender brought it to him he asked the man if he knew Dan Arcel.

"Sure, I know Arcel. He's a gambler."

"Has he been in town lately?"

"In and out."

"And now?"

The man thought a moment. He was very tall, balding, with a perpetual look of resignation on his face. Life had dealt him a hand, and he was going to play it out until the end, taking what came.

"Out."

"Where?"

"Why do you want him?"

"He's a friend of mine."

"You law?"

"No, I'm just a friend."

"What's your name, friend?"

"Adams, Clint Adams."

The man's eyebrows went up. They were bushy,

and Clint wondered if they would soon fall out the way the hair on the man's head had.

"The Gunsmith?"

Clint made a face.

"Can you tell me where he is?"

"Sure."

Clint didn't know if the man's sudden cooperation was due to the fact that he recognized him, or because he'd heard Arcel speak of him.

"He's at a private game."

That made sense. Arcel gambled for a living, and he certainly couldn't live on what he made at the Jericho Flats game twice a year. In addition to picking up games in saloons, Clint knew that the man had any number of private games that he took part in.

"Where?"

"Out at the McNee place."

"McNee?"

"John McNee. He's got a spread about five miles north of town. Raises horses, and hosts a private game."

"How often is this game played?"

"It *is* more than it isn't," the bartender said with a grin. "As long as he's got enough players, he's got a game. Fact is, even McNee don't play all the time, but he still holds the game."

"Five miles, you said?"

"Give or take a half."

Clint took out twice the price of the beer and tossed it on the bar.

"Thanks."

"Sure thing. You going out there to play?"

"Not exactly."

Clint left the saloon and stopped right outside the doors to consider his next move. He didn't want to wake Mickey, and he didn't want to take Duke right back out again without letting him rest. He decided to go over to the telegraph office and find out if Rick had any more information about Ed Ransom, or the others. After that he'd wake Mickey, feed her, and then put her back in the hotel while he checked out the game at the McNee place.

The Killer sat his horse on a rise, looking down at Amarillo. He knew where the McNee private game was held, and knew that Dan Arcel would be there. What he didn't know was when Arcel would be coming out. He didn't want to go into town and wait, because he didn't want to be seen, so he decided that he'd ride out to the McNee place, find a likely place to hole up from where he could see the house, and wait for Arcel to come out. The gambler couldn't sit still for more than two or three days, and would be ready to move on shortly.

That was when the Killer would make his move.

SEVEN

It was not as easy to convince Mickey to stay behind a second time, but the same argument finally prevailed. It also helped that, after eating, she seemed to succumb to fatigue again. She would go back to her room and go to sleep.

Clint had been unable to get anything useful from the telegraph office, but had wired Rick to keep trying.

Clint walked her to the hotel and then spoke to her sternly.

"I'm not kidding about this, Mickey. Stay in your room and wait for me. If you come out I'll ship you back to Labyrinth and have Rick Hartman sit on you. Understood?"

"I understand, Clint."

"All right. I should be back later this evening."

"If I'm asleep, please wake me and let me know. I don't want to wake up in the middle of the night and be afr—and wonder if you came back. All right?"

"All right, I'll wake you."

He watched her while she went up the steps, and then walked to the livery. He'd decided to rent a horse and leave Duke behind so he'd be well rested enough in the morning to travel.

He rented a likely-looking roan and headed out to the McNee ranch.

As Clint Adams approached the McNee ranch the

Killer, from his excellent vantage, recognized the Gunsmith. The man's heart began to beat a little faster, but he pushed any signs of panic aside. He could still do what he came to do and get away if he stayed calm.

Damn Clint Adams, anyway! He was supposed to be otherwise occupied.

As Clint rode up to the ranch house he saw the string of horses in the corral and noticed that they were of fine stock. Aside from running a game, McNee seemed to know what he was doing as far as raising horses was concerned.

He rode up to the corral where a man leaned on a fence post, waiting.

"Hello," Clint said.

"Howdy. Can I help you?"

"I'm looking for Dan Arcel."

"Don't know him."

The man was built solidly, low to the ground, with thick thighs and arms. He was in his thirties and looked as if he'd be formidable in a fistfight—with a grizzly!

"What's your name?"

"Vantana. I'm the foreman here."

"Well, Mr. Vantana, my name is Clint Adams. Dan Arcel is a friend of mine. I know he's here playing in Mr. McNee's private poker game, and I would like to see him. If you'd send someone inside to tell him that, I'm sure you'd get the okay to let me in."

Vantana studied Clint closely for a few moments. If he'd recognized the name he gave no indication.

Slowly, the foreman's heavily muscled arm came up and he signaled to someone. A man came running up and Vantana spoke to him briefly, speaking so that Clint could not hear. The man nodded and ran off.

"Nice-looking string," Clint said, nodding at the horses.

"They'll do," Vantana said, and that was the extent of the small talk they exchanged while awaiting word from inside.

Finally, the messenger returned, with another man following. From the look of the man—mid-fifties, but fit and prosperous looking—Clint assumed that this was John McNee himself.

"Mr. McNee," Vantana said. He seemed surprised to see his employer and stood up straight, abandoning the fence post.

"Vantana," the man said, nodding. He turned to look up at Clint and said, "You are Clint Adams?"

"I am."

"Step down, sir," McNee said. "I'd very much like to shake your hand."

Clint dismounted, trying to place the man's accent. If he was right, it was British.

They shook hands and McNee said, "It's a very great honor to meet you, sir. I've heard much about you."

"Don't believe all of it," Clint said.

"Ah, I know how reputations can be exaggerated, Mr. Adams, but the people I've heard of you from are not prone to such exaggerations."

"What people would those be?"

"Well, Dan Arcel for one. Beverly Press, for another."

Clint was surprised.

"You know Mrs. Press?"

"We have done business in the past. I ramrodded a drive for her, recently, with great success."

"It was a new experience." [1]

Beverly Press was a special friend of Clint's who

---

[1] The Gunsmith #59: The Trail Drive War.

lived in Wyoming, where she had a ranch. She also had a marvelous white stallion she called Lancelot, which she had loaned to Clint on two occasions. Actually, she had given Clint much more than a horse.

"This is certainly not the incredible black gelding I have heard so much about."

"No," Clint said, handing the reins to the man who had acted as messenger. "Duke is in the livery. We just arrived today and I want him to be well rested. We'll be leaving tomorrow morning."

"I'm very sorry to hear that," McNee said. "I was hoping to persuade you to stay and play—or at least to stay long enough for me to see this wonderful animal of yours."

"I'm sorry, but I do have pressing business elsewhere."

"Ah, if that is the case, then the business you have with Dan Arcel must be fairly serious."

"It is."

"You will come inside, then, and speak to him."

"I'd really rather not disrupt your game," Clint said, even though he was curious about who was playing. "Could you ask him to step outside?"

"As you wish. This way, please?"

McNee led Clint to the front door, where he waited while the man went inside to get Arcel.

Clint waited at the base of the steps that led to the front door, and as the door opened again and Dan Arcel stepped out, he turned.

Arcel said, "Clint—" smiling, already poised to come down the steps when the bullet hit him.

Clint heard the bullet strike Arcel in the center of the chest with a wet, smacking sound, and then the sound of the shot came afterward, firing from far off.

A hell of a shot, he thought, as he turned to try in

vain to see where it came from even as Arcel was
tumbling down the steps.

Clint caught Arcel as he reached the bottom step,
but from the look of the wound and the man's face,
he knew there was nothing anyone could do. The
weapon used had been a high-powered, large caliber
rifle. It was meant to fire a killing shot from hundreds of yards off, and that was just what it had
done.

Vantana came running over from the corral, and
McNee came charging out the front door.

"What happened?" he demanded. The way he
looked at Clint, he might have suspected the Gunsmith of luring Arcel outside so he could kill him.

"I saw it, Mr. McNee. Somebody fired a rifle from
a long way off and killed Arcel. It was some shot!"

Clint eased Arcel to the ground, stood up, and
once again looked off into the distance.

"Impossible to tell where it was fired from," he
said, half to himself. He looked down at Arcel and
then said with feeling, "Goddamn!"

EIGHT

Clint waited at the ranch while a man was sent to town for the sheriff. When the lawman arrived he was introduced by McNee as Sheriff Lawrence Black. Black was a man in his early forties who looked capable enough. The tip-off was the way he and McNee addressed each other, with mutual respect.

"John."

"Hello, Lawrence. This is Mr. Clint Adams. Mr. Adams, our sheriff, Lawrence Black."

Even in the face of violent death, McNee did not lose his well-mannered veneer.

"Care to tell me what happened here, Mr. Adams?"

While the sheriff listened, Clint explained what had just occurred. At one point, the lawman stared off into the distance, as if looking for some clue as to where the shot might have come from. As Clint spoke, the body was lifted onto a buckboard that had been supplied by McNee.

"John, can we have some of your men ride out and look for some sign?"

"Certainly. Vantana?"

"I'll take care of it, sir," the foreman said.

"Would you gentlemen care to go inside?" McNee asked.

"I think out here is good enough, John."

The sheriff obviously didn't want to interrupt McNee's game, either.

"All right with you?" Black asked Clint.

"Fine."

"Would you care to tell me why you were out here looking for this man, Arcel?"

Clint decided there was no point in holding anything back. He told Black the whole story.

"So you were out here to warn him."

"Right."

"Any chance you were followed?"

That was a cheerful thought. Had he led the killer right to Arcel?

"I don't think so. There was no reason for the killer to follow me. Besides, if he was that close to me why not just kill me?"

"Maybe he figured you'd lead him to the men he couldn't find. Or maybe you're not an intended target."

"Why the others and not me?"

"It may not be all of the others. You said yourself you haven't been able to contact some of the other players. Maybe the killer is after certain people, and not all of you."

"Possible," Clint said, but that would only make it even harder to figure out why.

"Am I free to go, Sheriff? I do have a fourteen-year-old girl in town waiting for me at the hotel. I don't want her to start to panic."

"Sure, I'm done. Vantana clears you of this. When are you leaving?"

"In the morning. I want to get the girl back to her father."

Black nodded.

"If I need you I'll find you in Jericho Flats?"

"Eventually."

"Why eventually?"

"I'm still hoping to locate some of the others and warn them, but I'll end up in Jericho Flats."

"Good enough," the sheriff said. "Care to ride back with us?"

McNee had supplied a man to drive the buckboard bearing Arcel's body back to town.

"I'll ride ahead, if you don't mind." It was getting near dark.

"Have it your way, but do me a favor, will you?"

"What's that?"

"Stop in and see me in the morning before you leave?"

"Sure thing." Clint turned to McNee and said, "I'm sorry this had to happen out here."

"No fault of yours, Mr. Adams. I'm sorry we did not meet under better circumstances."

Clint's horse was brought to him and he mounted up.

"Might be safer for you to ride back with us," the sheriff pointed out.

"If he wanted me he could have had me just as easily," Clint said. "That was an expert shot."

"You know anybody who could make a shot like that?"

"That's the problem, Sheriff," Clint said. "I know too many men who could make a shot like that."

NINE

It was late when Clint got back to town, and he went directly to Mickey's room. She was fourteen, after all, more than a child, less than a woman, and entitled to know what had happened. She was knuckling her eyes when she opened the door.

"Clint?"

"I'm back, honey," he said. "Let's go inside."

She backed up to let him in and he closed the door. She went back to the bed and got under the covers. In that moment she looked like a small child rather than a fourteen-year-old approaching womanhood.

"Bad news, Mickey," he said, and told her what had happened to Arcel.

"I'm sorry," she said. "He was a nice man."

"In light of this, Mickey, I think you should think about going back to Labyrinth."

"Why?"

"Well, there's a possibility the Killer followed us here," he explained. "If that's true, then he's liable to follow us tomorrow, as well."

"If he was following us, why didn't he just kill you, then?"

He explained the several views on that.

"Then he may not want to kill my pa?"

"That's a possibility."

"I've got to get to Jericho Flats, Clint. Please don't make me go back."

He regarded her for a few moments then said, "All right, honey. Go back to sleep and we'll leave in the morning."

"You won't leave without me, will you?"

"I wouldn't leave you here alone, Mickey."

She grinned and said, "Besides, you know I'd follow you."

"That's right," he said, "you would. If you need anything just knock on that wall," he said, pointing. "I'll be right next door."

"All right."

"Good night."

He left and went back to his own room. As he turned down the bed he realized how truly tired he was, and it didn't help to have had a man who was very nearly a friend gunned down in front of him.

The killer had balls, he had to give him that. To have camped himself outside McNee's ranch, waiting for a shot at that distance took guts—and to make the shot, that took talent. As Clint had told Sheriff Black, he knew a lot of men—and some women—who could have made that shot, but none of them would have had a motive. None of them had ever been in Jericho Flats, as far as he knew.

Clint was at a loss to figure it all out right at that moment. He didn't have enough information—and he was too damned tired to think about it anymore.

The last thing he remembered he was trying to take off his boots. When he awoke the next morning, he still had one on.

The Killer knew he had several options.

He could wait for morning, let Clint Adams leave Amarillo, and follow him, but he didn't think Clint knew where Ed Ransom was.

The Killer, on the other hand, did.

His best bet was to go on ahead and take care of

Ransom, and then get to Jericho Flats before Adams and Mickey.

He could also kill the Gunsmith from a distance, as he had done with Arcel, but there really wasn't any need for that—not yet, anyway. If he had to take care of the Gunsmith, he could always do it later on.

Right now he wanted to stick to his schedule.

And Ed Ransom was next.

His third option was less desirable.

He could forget all about this "mission" he was on and go back home, leave the others alive. They'd never find out who killed Kelly, Jennings, Collins, and Arcel. In point of fact, he was safe now, even without killing the rest—but he knew he couldn't stop. He started this, and he had to finish it cleanly. If he left one of them alive, there was a chance that one would figure it out.

He wasn't happy with the course of action he had chosen, but he had thought long and hard before choosing it, and had done so because he truly believed that there was no other way.

No, he'd dealt himself this hand, and he had to play it without any bottom dealing to get himself out of it.

TEN

In the morning Clint and Mickey went for breakfast at the same place they'd had dinner the night before. Dinner had been terrible, but Clint figured how badly could they mess up eggs?

"What are we going to do now?" Mickey asked. "Look for Mr. Ransom?"

"No," Clint said. "I'd have no idea where to look. We'll head for Jericho Flats. Somewhere along the way I'll check in with Rick again, to see if he's come up with anything. If not, we'll just get to your father that much faster."

"I want to get to him as fast as possible, but I'd also like to be able to warn Mr. Ransom."

"We will if we can, Mickey."

After breakfast Clint took Mickey with him to the sheriff's office.

"Good morning, Adams," Sheriff Black said.

" 'Morning, Sheriff. This is Mickey Reynolds."

"Hello, Mickey."

"Sheriff."

"Adams, I've been wondering what to do with Arcel's personal belongings. Did he have any relatives?"

"Not that I know of."

"I guess I could have everything buried with him—that is, unless you want his things."

51

Clint was about to decline when he suddenly thought better of it.

"I think I would like to have them, Sheriff."

"All right."

The sheriff reached down next to his desk and brought up a canvas sack that was more empty than filled.

"Is his wallet in there?" Clint asked.

"Yes," the sheriff said, reaching in and producing it.

Clint took it, fanned it open, and removed all the cash inside. Without counting it—and he knew that it would be substantial—he handed it to Black.

"What's this for?" the lawman asked, as if ready to take offense.

"Use whatever you have to to give him a good burial, and then drop the rest off at the saloon and let the customers drink it up. Tell them that the drinks are on Dan Arcel."

The sheriff looked at the money in his hand, and then opened a drawer and put it in his desk. For some reason Clint was sure that the man would do the right thing, and would not keep the money himself.

"I'll take care of it."

"All right."

"Before you leave town, is there anything else you could tell me that might shed some light on this?"

"I thought about it all last night, Sheriff, and I don't mind telling you that I'm baffled—but I can promise you one thing."

"What's that?"

"When I do find out who killed him, and the others, I'll let you know."

"Well, maybe this will help," Black said. He took a small envelope out of his shirt pocket and handed it to Clint.

"What's this?"

"Telegram came for you last night, as the operator was closing up. I saw him in the street, and since it was late he gave it to me."

"Have you read it?"

The lawman returned Clint's steady gaze and said, "No, I haven't."

Even though the envelope was sealed, the sheriff still could have read it—it could have been read and resealed very easily. Still, Clint decided to believe him. He had a feeling about Sheriff Black, and he was usually a good judge of character.

He opened it and read it.

"What is it?" Mickey asked.

"It's from Rick. He's located Ed Ransom."

"One of the other men?" Black asked.

"Yes."

"Where—wait a minute. On second thought, don't tell me where he is. It might be better that way."

"I agree," Clint said, putting the telegram away. He and the sheriff shook hands and said good-bye.

Outside, Mickey asked, "Where is he, Clint?"

"Colorado," Clint said. "We can stop on the way to Jericho Flats and try to warn him—if we're in time."

ELEVEN

On the way to Colorado Clint told Mickey how Rick Hartman had found out where Ed Ransom was.

"It seems Ransom ran out of money and had to wire his home office for some. Well, Rick happened to get in touch with the home office, and they told him where they were sending the money."

"Colorado?"

"Right. A town called Red Gate."

"I wonder why they called it that?"

A week later, they found out when they came to a signpost with a red gate attached to it. The sign said—naturally—RED GATE, 1 MILE.

"Do you think he'll still be here?" Mickey asked.

"If he's not, maybe they can tell us where he went, or which way he headed. In any case, let's not give ourselves problems we don't have. Come on."

When they rode into Red Gate they found a moderately sized town that didn't really look as if it would go much further in the way of growth. There was no new construction visible, as if the people were satisfied with what they had.

"There's the telegraph office," Clint said. "And the sheriff's office. We'll put the horses up in the livery and check back."

The first place they stopped was the telegraph office. Inside, Clint described Ransom to the clerk, who nodded, rubbing his jaw.

"Don't need to describe him," the sixtyish clerk said, "I remember the man. Desperate, he was, for that money."

"Would you know why?"

"Everyone knew why," the old man said. "He got hisself into a poker game over at the saloon and needed the money to keep playing. Yeah, everybody knew that—everybody but his company."

"Would you know where he is now?"

The man frowned and said, "Reckon you better ask the sheriff that question, young feller."

"Why?" Mickey asked.

The old man looked at Mickey over the top of his wire-framed glasses and said, "Like I said, young lady. Go and ask the sheriff."

"Come on, Mickey," Clint said. "That was our next stop, anyway."

Clint steered Mickey out of the telegraph office and to the sheriff's office, which was across the street. He knocked on the door and they entered.

The man seated behind the desk looked more like a schoolteacher than a sheriff. He was tall, dark-haired, smooth-faced, wearing a dark suit with a white shirt, like he was all set to address his class.

"Sheriff?" Clint asked.

"That's right," the man said, standing up. "Sheriff Howard Kellerman. What can I do for you, sir?"

"My name is Clint Adams, Sheriff, and this is Mickey Reynolds."

"Pleased to meet you, miss," the sheriff said. "How can I help you?"

"We're looking for a man named Ed Ransom, who was in your town a little over a week ago."

"Ransom?"

"That's right. He's a salesman, but as I understand he got himself involved in a big poker game over at the hotel and had to send away to his company for some money. That's how we tracked him down, here."

"Tracked him down?" the sheriff said. "Are you a bounty hunter, Mr. Adams."

"Don't you even recognize—" Mickey started, but Clint put a hand on her shoulder to quiet her.

"No, Sheriff, I'm not a bounty hunter. I'm a friend of Ed Ransom's, and I'm trying to get to him to warn him that his life might be in danger."

"From who?"

"We don't know that," Clint said. "All we know is that several people are dead and we have reason to believe that Ed Ransom could be next. Do you know where he is?"

"Sure do."

"Good. Where?"

"He was over by the undertaker's, but he must be buried by now."

"Buried?"

"That's right. You don't have to worry about his life being in danger anymore. Somebody killed him last week."

TWELVE

"Did you notify his company?"

"We did, but we never got a reply."

Probably got tired of sending him money and decided he got what he deserved, Clint thought. He turned to the sheriff and asked, "How did he die?"

"He was shot in the alley by his hotel."

"From where? By who?"

"Don't know who, and I figure whoever it was was on the roof of the hotel. Blew a hole in him as he was approaching the hotel to go to his room, I guess."

"What kind of weapon was used?"

"Rifle."

"A high-powered rifle?"

"Why would anyone need a high-powered rifle for a shot from the roof of the hotel?"

"Was it a large caliber?"

"Not particularly. In fact, it could have been a handgun, if the shooter was good enough."

If it was the man Clint was thinking of, he would have been good enough.

"Have you questioned anyone?"

"Questioned the men he was playing cards with. Seems that when he got that extra money from his company he started a pretty good winning streak."

"You think any of the players killed him?"

"Doesn't figure. They were all together at the

saloon, still playing, when he was shot."

"Would you mind if I spoke to them?"

"What for?"

"Personal satisfaction." Before Clint assumed that Ransom was killed by the same man who killed the others, he wanted to satisfy himself that he wasn't killed because of something that had happened in the poker game.

"No, I guess not."

"How many players were involved?"

"Four others. I can arrange for you to speak with them, if you want."

"I'd appreciate it."

"Why don't you get yourself a drink and then come back?"

"We'll get something to eat," Clint said, "if you'll tell us a likely place."

The sheriff gave them directions to a restaurant, and they agreed to meet back at the sheriff's office in an hour.

"If I don't have the people here, I'll be able to bring them to you."

"Fine."

Clint and Mickey left the sheriff's office and Mickey started in the direction of the restaurant.

"Are you coming?" she asked when Clint made no move to follow her.

"Do you have any money?" Clint asked her.

"No."

"Here," he said, giving her some. "Get something to eat and then meet me at the livery in an hour and a half."

"What?"

"Get going."

"What do I do if you don't show up?"

"Just wait."

"Clint, is something wrong?"

"I don't know," Clint said, "but I intend to find out."

There was something about the sheriff and his pat answers that Clint didn't like. He felt that something wasn't right, and this was pure hunch country. He had absolutely no facts to go on, but he hoped to get some by following the sheriff.

He stood in a doorway across the street and waited ten minutes before the sheriff came out and walked hurriedly in the opposite direction from the one Mickey had taken. That made sense. If he had some arrangements to make in the north end of town, he'd send Clint Adams to the south end of town to eat.

Clint followed the sheriff as the man made four stops, and then returned to his office. After that Clint went over to look at the hotel and the alley where Ransom had been shot. He waited until the other four men had joined the sheriff, and then crossed the street and entered the office.

Time for the game to begin.

THIRTEEN

"Mr. Adams. Right on time," the sheriff said.

"Are these the men who played in the high stakes poker game with Ed Ransom?"

"This is them."

"But we didn't kill him," one man said nervously.

"How would you know?" Clint asked.

"What?"

"How would you know if one of these other men killed him or not."

The man gave Clint a belligerent look and said, "Because we was together the whole time, that's why."

"Is that what the sheriff told you to say?"

"Sure—hey, wha—?" the man said, looking at the sheriff.

"What are you trying to say here, Adams?"

"Come on, Sheriff. This man is a clerk in the general store. This one works as a teller in the bank. That one there works as a clerk in the hardware store, and this one here with all the answers, he's probably a swamper at the saloon. You dressed him up some, but you can still smell him."

"Hey!" the man in question said.

"You followed me," the sheriff said accusingly.

"That's right."

"Well—"

"Well," Clint said. "You want to try explaining, or should I?"

"I just didn't want you bothering the other players in the game. They're all prominent men."

"Yeah," one man, the teller, said. "My boss is real busy—"

"Shut up, Elmo!" Sheriff Kellerman shouted.

"Get rid of them, Sheriff," Clint said. "We don't need them anymore."

The sheriff jerked his head at the four men and they got up and left.

"You killed Ransom and took his money. You planned it when you found out he was the big winner in the game."

"No!" the sheriff shouted. "That's not what happened."

"Then you tell me what happened, and make me believe you."

"I—I saw how much he won at the game and I followed him. Nobody was around so I hit him, dragged him into the alley and took his money—but he was alive when I left the alley."

"How was he shot?"

"Through the chest, probably at close range with a handgun. Somebody killed him after I left him there, and that's the truth."

"What did you do with the money?"

"I still have it."

"Hand it over," Clint said, putting out his hand.

For a moment the sheriff looked like he was sizing Clint up.

"Don't make a mistake that would definitely be your last, Howard."

The sheriff opened a drawer in his desk and took out a thick brown envelope. He handed it to Clint who, judging from the width, wasn't surprised that the sheriff had done what he'd done.

"I'll take the rest of his belongings, too."

"The undertaker has them."

"Fine."

"What now?" the sheriff asked.

"You resign. I'm going to turn this over to some-one in town, without telling you who. I'll tell them the whole story—"

"It's my word against yours!"

"If I find out you haven't resigned, I'll come back and resign you—permanently."

They exchanged stares, and eventually the sheriff lowered his eyes.

"Nice talking to you," Clint said, and left.

"I kept him here for a while to see if any kin could be found, but when he started to smell I had to bury him."

The speaker was a man named Judd White, the town undertaker. Why, Clint wondered, were all undertakers so tall and painfully thin?

"I even sent a wire to his company to see if they wanted to bury him, but I never got an answer. Do you want to see his grave?" White asked.

"No," Clint said, "that's not necessary. We've got to keep moving."

"Not staying overnight?"

"There's no need now," Clint said. "We found what we came for. Can I have his property, please?"

"Sure."

There wasn't much in the way of belongings, so Clint dumped it into the same sack with Arcel's things. It was only then that he realized he had never looked at Arcel's belongings. He decided that when they next stopped to camp he would examine both men's property.

"Oh, there's this," Clint said, passing the money over to the undertaker.

"What?" the man said, taking it.

"The dead man's money. Give him the best headstone you've got, and buy drinks for the house at the saloon with the rest—as many times as you can."

The man looked inside the envelope and said, "This'll keep the whole town drunk for a year."

"Might do 'em some good."

After they left the undertaker's Mickey said, "What if he keeps the money?"

"That's better than letting the sheriff have it."

"And who are you going to tell about the sheriff?"

"Nobody."

"But you told him—"

Clint looked at her and said, "I lied."

At the livery he saddled both Duke and Mickey's horse, and boosted Mickey up into the saddle. He settled with the liveryman, and they were on their way. They passed another red gate sign on the way out of town.

They also passed the town cemetery, so Clint decided just to ride over and see if he could spot Ransom's grave. It wasn't hard to spot. Most of the others had stone markers, while Ransom's grave just had a wooden cross with his last name crudely written on it: RANSOM.

"There'll be a stone there soon," Clint said, hoping that even if the undertaker did keep the money he'd at least give Ransom a stone for the donation.

"Did he have family?" Mickey asked.

"Damned if I know. All he ever talked about was his company, and now they don't want any part of him."

Mickey looked at Clint with some tears in her eyes and said, "We've got to get to Jericho Flats, Clint. We've really got to get there . . . before . . ."

"I know, honey," he said. "I know. That's where we're headed right now!"

The trip through Colorado to Wyoming was uneventful. Nobody made a try for them, and as far as Clint could tell nobody was following them.

They were camped about two days' ride out of Jericho Flats when he suddenly realized that he still had not gone through the personal possessions of Arcel and Ransom.

"What are you doing?" she asked as he stood up.

"I want to get something."

He went to get the sack, which he'd left next to Duke, and brought it back to the fire. He sat down and dumped it all out onto the ground.

"Arcel and Ransom's property," he said, poking through it.

"What are you looking for?"

"I don't know. Maybe something that will tell me why they're both dead."

"Can I help?"

"Sure. If you think you've found something, just sing out."

They divided the pile in half, both men's property being all mixed in, and began looking: reading papers, looking at photos. Clint picked up Arcel's wallet and picked through it. No money, of course —but then he saw a tear and a flash of green. Looking closer he could see that someone had torn the inside of the wallet, revealing a hidden one-thousand-dollar bill? Why hadn't the bill been taken?

"What did you find?" she asked.

"A thousand dollars."

"Really?"

"Hidden away in a small compartment. Somebody tore the inside of the wallet apart looking for something."

"Looking for what?"

"I don't know, but they didn't take the thousand-dollar bill."

"Why not?"

"It's not surprising. They left all of his money anyway, so why take a hidden thousand dollars. The question is, what else was hidden in here, and why was *it* taken?" He put the wallet down and said, "Mickey, give me Ransom's wallet."

"I looked through it already," she said, handing it to him.

"I know, but now let's look for something hidden."

He leafed through the wallet as she had, then began looking for a secret compartment. He did find a small flap where something could have been hidden, but it was empty. Whether or not there ever was something there could not be determined.

"Something could have been here," he said, dropping the wallet back into the pile, "but there's no way of knowing."

"So what do we do now?"

"I don't know. I'm convinced that Arcel had something hidden with his thousand dollars, but what?"

"A piece of paper?"

"With what written on it?"

"The name of his killer?"

"Maybe," Clint said, "without realizing that it was the name of the person who would become his killer."

Idly, Clint flipped through the rest of the stuff,

and then began tossing photos and papers into the fire.

He was left with the wallets, the thousand-dollar bill, Arcel's .22 caliber derringer and Ransom's .36 Navy Colt—though why he carried a monster gun like that Clint could only guess.

"Neither of them had any family?"

"None alive," Clint said, indicating the burning photos in the fire.

"My pa's the only family I have alive," Mickey said. "What if he's already dead, Clint?"

"What?" Clint said, because the question had come out of nowhere.

"What if my pa's already dead when we get there. What do I do then?"

"He won't be."

"What if he is?"

Clint stared at Mickey across the fire, then decided to tell her something that he had been thinking.

"There are two reasons I can think of that your father won't be dead when we get to town, Mickey, either one of which could be true."

"What are they?"

"Number one, the Killer might only be after certain players. He's killed five of them now, and he never made a try for me, even though I was that close to Arcel. He might be finished."

"What's the other reason?"

"If he's after all the players," Clint said, "it would make sense to me for him to leave your father for last."

"Why?"

"Because your father started the Jericho Flats game, and if it's the Killer's plan to kill all the players, he'd leave the man who started the whole thing for last."

He put the remains of the two dead men's belongings back into the sack and set it aside. The hidden compartment in the wallet still bothered him.

She stared at him, digesting everything he had just said.

"Feel any better?" he asked.

She stared at him, then looked into the fire and said, "No . . . but thanks anyway."

FOURTEEN

Jericho Flats was not a big town. Clint often felt that that was why Jock Reynolds had settled there, opened his business, and started his game. Almost all of it could go unnoticed.

Nobody who knew Jock knew where his money came from. It certainly didn't come from running the town's only livery stable, or from being the town blacksmith, yet these were the only professions he seemed to have.

As they rode down the main street toward the livery—Jock's Livery—Clint wondered if even Mickey knew.

They rode up to the livery and saw that the front doors were closed.

"He should be open," Mickey said worriedly.

"He owns the place, Mickey," Clint said. "He can close whenever he wants to."

"I suppose."

Clint dismounted and as Mickey began to do the same he said, "Stay up there."

"Why?"

Clint shrugged.

"I just want to have a look around."

Mickey looked as if she would protest, then sat back down on her saddle and said, "All right."

Clint went to the front doors and pulled on them, but they were locked.

71

"Go around the side. There's a key underneath the barrel by the door."

"Right."

Clint walked around the livery and found the side door. It was the door they all used when they came for the game. He tipped up the barrel by the door—it was empty—found the key, unlocked the door, and then put the key back. He stepped in and found himself in darkness. He took a few steps and then saw the light toward the back of the building. Jock's office.

He walked toward the light and saw that the door was ajar. Slowly, as quietly as he could, he approached the door and pushed it open.

Jock Reynolds whirled on him, a .45 held out in front of him, aimed right at the Gunsmith.

"Whoa!" Clint said.

"Jesus Christ!" Jock said. He lowered the gun, shook his head, and said, "Jesus Christ" again.

Behind Reynolds was his desk, and over the desk on the wall were several rifles. One was a Sharps Big Fifty—indicating that Jock might have been a buffalo hunter at one time—another was a lever action Henry, and the third a Winchester '73.

"Clint Adams, what in the Sam Hill are you doing here? You're supposed to be in Texas."

"Texas got boring."

"It did, huh— Hey, where's Michelle?"

"She's outside."

"You brought her back?"

"More like she brought me."

Jock Reynolds stood up. He was a big man, six three or so, as wide and hairy a man as Clint had ever seen. He wasn't muscular, but he was thick, and Clint had seen him put many a muscleman down with a swipe of one huge arm.

He hoped he wasn't about to face one of those arms.

"Jock—"

"Let's get that front door open and let her in. Then we'll talk."

"Right."

They went to the front doors, unlocked them, and swung them open. The inside became brilliantly lit and Mickey came riding in leading Duke behind her.

"Pa!" she cried as Jock lifted her from her saddle and hugged her close.

"Pa, I was so worried."

"Why'd you come back, Michelle?"

"I just told you, Pa," she said as he put her down, "I was worried."

"Yeah," Jock said, "So was I—about you."

Jock looked at Clint who shrugged and said, "She wouldn't stay put, Jock. She's stubborn."

"Like her mother was."

"And her father," Clint said.

Jock looked at Clint, and then his granite face split into a grin and he said, "Yeah. You want a drink?"

"I thought you'd never ask."

They closed the front doors, shrouding the place in darkness again, then lit a couple of lamps and went back to Jock's office. Mickey sat real close to her pa while he and Clint passed a bottle back and forth.

"So, they got Arcel and Ransom, too."

"Before I could get to them. They—he—whoever it is, got Arcel right in front of me," Clint said. "That's what galls me!"

"So who's left?"

"Bat Masterson, Luke Short, Tal Roper, you and me," Clint said.

"Not an easy bunch to put away," Jock commented. "What about players who left the game?"

"What about them?"

"There's a few, you know. Miller Riley, Jason Warden, Steve Shay."

"Also not easy to put away—but then neither was Joe Kelly."

"Kelly was first, wasn't he?"

"Yeah, but that's a while back now."

"Could that be a coincidence, and not part of this?"

"They could all be coincidence, Jock," Clint said. "Do you want to believe that?"

"Do I want to, yes," Jock said. "Ask me if I do, and the answer is no."

"Do you know where the others are?"

"I got an idea, yeah."

"Why would somebody want to kill them?" Mickey asked.

"Honey," Clint said, "we don't know why anyone would want to kill any of us, but they were part of this game at one time. We owe them a warning."

"If they're still alive," Jock said.

"This ragtag town still got a telegraph office?" Clint asked.

"Yeah."

"Well, let's get to it, then," Clint said, standing up. "If they are still alive, we want to keep them that way."

Jock put the bottle aside and stood up.

"Why don't you get yourself settled at the hotel. I'll take care of the telegrams."

"That sounds good. After that we can get something to eat."

"You both come to the house and I'll cook," Mickey said.

Clint looked at her and said, "That sounds like a fine idea, Mickey."

"You come with me to the telegraph office, honey, and then we'll go to the house and meet Clint."

"All right, Pa."

"I'll take care of Duke before I leave," Jock said.

"I'll see you at the house, Jock."

Clint left the livery the same way he had come. Maybe it was a good idea to bring Mickey back, after all. They could both look after her here.

At least they'd eat good.

FIFTEEN

Jock Reynolds's home was a wood frame, one-story house right next to the livery. Over dinner Clint and Jock discussed everything they had done to this point, and what they would do now that they were together.

Jock had also been sending telegrams in an attempt to warn Bat, Luke, and Tal Roper, but he'd had the same luck that Clint had.

"I'm doing the same thing with the other three now, Riley, Warden, and Shay. I've got a general idea where they are, and I've sent telegrams trying to track them down."

"I'd like to find out if they're alive. It would help us figure out this killer's next move."

"If he's only after active players in the game, that leaves five targets. If he's after all of us, then he's got eight."

"Right."

"What are we going to do now, Clint? Sit here and wait for him to get to us?"

"If we're having trouble finding the others, maybe he is, too," Clint suggested. "Maybe he'll come here, figuring that you're a stationary target."

"That would make sense. Even if he was saving me for last, he might do that just to get me out of the way."

"Please . . ." Mickey said. She'd been silent up to that point.

"I'm sorry, honey," Jock said, covering her hand with his. "We've got to face facts, though."

"I know, I know," she said.

"Clint, maybe you should ride out and try to find the others?"

"That would take forever, even if I traveled by stage and by train. No, I think I'd rather stay here and wait for the Killer to show up."

"That could take forever, too."

"Maybe you could make me a partner?"

"You wouldn't like the hours," Jock said, and directed his attention to his meal.

It was a delicious meal—beef stew in a rich and thick gravy, with huge lumps of potato and vegetables and soft biscuits—but it didn't require as much attention as Jock was giving it now. A simple remark about his "business" and the big man closed up tight.

When he had come here to play cards Clint had never really wondered where Jock's money came from. In the beginning, yes, he had been curious about where a livery stable owner got the money to not only play in a high stakes poker game, but to be the one who held the game.

Now that he was here in Jericho Flats for an unknown amount of time, his curiosity began to surface again.

After the meal Clint stood up and said, "That was wonderful, Mickey."

"Thank you."

"Jock, I think I'll go over to the saloon for a while."

"I'll join you later. Michelle's been away for a while and I want to catch up."

"Okay. Good night, Mickey."

"Good night, Clint."

Clint left and went over to Jericho Flat's largest saloon, the China Clipper. It was owned and operated by an ex-sailor who had long since given up the sea for dry ground, but had fashioned the place after a schooner. Even the batwing doors had portholes in them.

Clint entered and walked to the bar. On the wall behind it were hanging all sorts of seafaring articles, from harpoons to a huge anchor that the owner —Captain Jack Thatcher—said had been used on every ship he'd ever owned.

Captain Jack was tending bar, a black patch over his left eye. Clint had never been able to find out if he really needed it, or if he just wore it for effect.

"Clint Adams is it," he bellowed, "or is me eye deceiving me?"

"It's me all right, Captain Jack."

Grizzled was the only word that could be used to describe the saloon owner. He rarely shaved, yet always seemed to have stubble rather than a beard. His hair was white, his single eye a blue that sparkled with mischief, and when he smiled his mouth revealed teeth like headstones.

"Well, shiver me timbers, lad, and what'll ye have?"

"Beer."

"Comin' up."

Jack brought the beer and leaned his bony elbows on the bar.

"And what brings ye this way, lad?"

"Just visiting."

"Well, t'isn't July and t'isn't January, but would you still be visitin' yer old friend Jock Reynolds?"

"I would."

"Trouble a-brewin', lad?"

Clint sipped his beer and set the mug down.

"Why would you say that, Captain?"

Jack shrugged shoulders that were easily as bony as his elbows.

"Just a wild guess."

"Too wild."

"Well, just so's ye know that if trouble does rear its ugly head, ye can count on Captain Jack."

"I'll remember that."

"Customers a-callin'. Be seein' ye later, lad."

Clint turned around to face the rest of the room and sipped his beer. The appeal of Captain Jack was obvious and simple: drink and women. If it was gambling you wanted, you had to get up your own game. Clint saw that there was a poker game in progress in a corner, a table with four players and five chairs. That fifth, empty chair was beckoning to him and he figured, why not?

Might as well make some money while he was in town.

SIXTEEN

An hour later, when Jock Reynolds entered the saloon, Clint was two hundred dollars ahead. He saw Jock as the big man entered, exchanged glances with him, and then Jock went to the bar.

Jock never played in saloon games. He saved himself for high stakes games. Clint, on the other hand, although he enjoyed playing for big stakes, also simply enjoyed playing.

He played another hour while Jock stood at the bar, downing beers. The man had a prodigious tolerance for beer and liquor.

There was another person in the saloon that Clint noticed. She was a tall, well-rounded redhead who was working the room, stopping at this table and that to exchange barbs and flirtatious remarks with customers, but she never once came near the poker table. Once, however, Clint caught her looking his way, and it was enough to tell him that the interest he felt was mutual.

There were three other girls working the room, but none of them attracted his attention the way she did. Had she not been there, he would have happily settled for any of the other three, for they were all attractive, and they were all looking his way.

This one, however, was there, so . . .

"That's it, boys," he said. "Time for me to quit."

"You got most of our money," one man said sourly.

"I'll be here tomorrow, friend, and you can win it back—if you can."

That seemed to mollify the man somewhat, and there were no further complaints when Clint picked up his money and left the table.

He walked to the bar and stood next to Jock, who had a beer waiting.

"I notice you and Darlene have spotted each other."

"Darlene?"

"The redhead."

"Have I ever seen her before?"

"You'd remember if you had."

"You've got that right."

Jock and Clint watched Darlene continue to work the room, and when she spotted Clint at the bar she walked over, hips swaying elaborately.

She was about five foot five, which gave Clint a fine vantage point of her creamy cleavage. Her eyes were green but, unlike other redheads that he had known, this one had nary a freckle on her face.

Of course, there was a lot of makeup . . .

"Finish your game?"

"For now. I appreciate you not coming over. It would have played hell with my concentration."

"That's a nice thing for you to say."

"I'm a nice guy."

Darlene looked at Jock who spread his hands and said, "Don't look at me. Find out for yourself—but I have to warn you about one thing."

"What's that?"

"In a saloon his money only comes out of his pockets for drink and cards."

She pouted and then brightened.

"Maybe we can do something about that later,

then, huh?'' she asked Clint.

"I think something can be worked out."

"After all," she said, turning to walk away, "a girl needs practice, too, right?"

As she left Captain Jack came over to enjoy the view with them and then said, "I'll warn ye now, lad, that one is my best money maker. Don't be takin' up her time during business hours."

"I wouldn't dream of it, Captain."

"Well, then, for yer promise I'll buy ye both a beer."

"And we'll accept."

"How did you do?" Jock asked.

"Won a little."

"Against that lot you can't do much else. Why do you bother with such small games?"

"I enjoy playing."

"You'll never make a lot of money that way."

"And how did you make all your money, Jock?" Clint asked, even before he realized he was going to ask.

"It wasn't from sitting in on penny ante games."

"You made it from poker, then?"

"A good portion of it."

"Moved here, opened your own business, and started your own game?"

"That's it."

"All of it?"

"Enough as I care to tell."

"But you didn't tell, I did. You just agreed."

"I don't go asking you how you make your money, Clint."

"You have a point there, Jock," Clint said, and dropped the subject, sorry he'd brought it up.

Jock finished his beer and said, "Well, I guess I'll be turning in. I want to check in at the telegraph office early in the morning. You fixed at the hotel?"

"I am."

Clint had not taken offense at not being asked by Jock to stay at his house. He had never heard Jock make the offer to anyone.

"See you in the morning, then."

"Yup. Good night."

As Jock left, Captain Jack came over and said, "Queer bird, that one."

"How so?"

"Got more money than any liveryman I ever knew."

"Spread that around, do you?"

"I do not," Jack said. "You bein' a friend of his and all, didn't see the harm in saying somethin' I been thinkin' for a long time, now . . ."

"And how many liverymen did you know on the high seas, Cap'n?"

"Don't be smart-mouthin' yer elders, laddie. Another beer?"

Clint's eyes followed Darlene and he said, "While I wait, why not?"

SEVENTEEN

As he had suspected, the makeup had hidden freckles.

"Grown women should not have freckles," Darlene said. She was seated before a mirror, removing her makeup.

"Redheads do."

"And you've known a lot of redheads, have you?" she asked, eyeing him through the mirror.

"Some."

"I'll bet."

They were in her room, a room she kept over the hardware store, not the one she had at the saloon. That was her paying room, she said. This was where she came when she wanted to be alone—or with someone special.

He was seated on her bed, watching her. The only thing he had removed was his gunbelt, which was hanging within easy reach on the bedpost.

Darlene had undressed behind a screen and donned a dressing robe. Clint could see her breasts moving beneath it, and the desire he'd begun to feel when he first saw her began to build. Being in the same room with her, smelling her, watching her remove her makeup and comb her hair, it was all combining to make staying dressed a painful experience. He shifted again to try to ease the pressure.

She smiled at him through the mirror and said,

"I'm making you wait, aren't I?"

"I don't mind."

"No, you really don't. Someone else would be full of demands, trying to get my robe off by now, but not you."

"I told you in the saloon," he said, "I'm a nice guy."

"Nice guys should be rewarded."

She stood up, turned, unbelted her gown, and dropped it to the floor.

"That's what I call a reward," he said.

She was full-bodied, and made no attempts to disguise it. That is, her belly was not flat and she did not hold her breath, trying to make it appear so. Her thighs were heavy, her breasts round and firm-looking, the sides pressing against each other. Her nipples were very dark and large.

She came to him and got down on her knees. She helped him with his boots and socks, then with his pants and underwear, and finally his shirt.

She fell back on her heels and looked at him. Sitting on the bed his erection was standing stiff and eager. She leaned forward and touched the swollen head with her tongue. She swirled it around, then licked him all the way down the shaft. He moved so that she could reach his balls, which she also laved with her tongue. She worked her way back up his shaft, then leaned forward, hands braced on his thighs, and took him into her mouth—slowly and fully!

Her head began to bob up and down then as she worked the length of him, wetting him and sucking him, moaning out her pleasure. There was no money involved here, so her pleasure was real. He knew that without a doubt.

At the point where he was ready to burst she allowed him to slide free, giving him one last, fleeting lick that almost set him off.

The bed had already been turned down and now she pushed him back onto the cool sheets. She got on the bed with him and dangled her breasts in his face. He grasped them in his hands and licked them, tasting the salt of her perspiration with pleasure. He sucked the nipples until they were fully distended, and then pushed her onto her back, changing positions with her.

He settled down between her legs and proceeded to do for her what she had done for him, use his tongue and his mouth to get her ready. She writhed on the bed, grinding her delicious bottom into the sheet as she came, and then reached for him and pulled him atop her.

He slid into her so easily, loving the heat that surrounded him. He began to move inside her and she groaned, moving with him, grabbing his buttocks and digging her nails into him.

When he exploded she opened her mouth and came with him, but no sound came out. He moaned as he emptied into her, and she buried her face into his neck and rode out the spasms with him, the bed squeaking in accompaniment to their erotic dance.

Later, as they were lying side by side, each replaying scenes in their minds, savoring them, preparing for the next one, she asked, "How long will you be staying in town?"

"I don't know. A few days, a few weeks . . ."

"A few months?" she asked, a hopeful note creeping into her voice.

"God forbid," he said, but she did not take offense. He had obviously known many women, just as she had known many men. This one, however, cared about her pleasure as much as he did his own. That made him different, and for that she wouldn't mind having him around for a while.

"Business?"

"A mixture of business and pleasure."

"You're friends with Jock?"

"Yes. Have you and Jock—"

"No. He doesn't come into the saloon for much other than drinking."

"Does he do that a lot?"

"Not an awful lot—not until recently, that is. Over the past month or so he's been in more often, drinking more than he used to."

"Has he been talking while drunk? Or getting into trouble?"

"No. He does get drunk, but then he just walks out and goes home. I mean, I assume he goes home." Suddenly, she rolled toward him and said, "Do we have to talk?"

"Don't you want to get to know each other?" he asked, teasing.

"I thought we just did that."

He rolled toward her so that their bodies were pressed together from chest to crotch and said, "Well, let's go over it again. There might have been something we missed."

Clint left Darlene during the night and went back to his own room. Something had happened during the night that had changed the mood between them, and although he couldn't put his finger on it, he knew it was there.

It would come to him.

EIGHTEEN

The next morning Clint went to Jock's house, where Mickey made them breakfast.

"Jock, I know that Bill Clark is the sheriff here in Jericho Flats, but I don't know much about him."

"Bill? He's been the law here for about three years. Before that he was deputy for two."

"What about before he came here?"

"He did some deputying here and about, nothing to write home about."

"What about his term as sheriff?"

"He's been a good lawman, the right kind for this town."

"What does that mean?"

"All he's got to handle here is some Saturday night drunks and their irate Sunday morning wives."

"If there's trouble heading this way, maybe he should be told about it. Get him ready to handle whatever comes."

Jock considered the suggestion.

"I suppose you're right, although I don't rightly know how he *would* handle it."

"Has he got any deputies?"

"Two—one full time, one part time."

"I think it's only right to let him know what's been going on."

"All right, then," Jock agreed. "We'll do that right after breakfast."

After breakfast Mickey brought them both another cup of coffee and Jock said, "Michelle, why don't you get started on your chores?"

"I have to wash the cups when you're done."

"Don't worry about that. Clint and I are capable of washing a couple of cups."

"All right, Pa." She flashed Clint a smile, took off her apron, and was gone.

"Why'd you send her away?" Clint asked.

"Two reasons. Number one, she thinks she's in love with you."

"She's a kid."

"She's almost a woman, Clint. I don't want her getting hurt."

"I wouldn't hurt her, Jock. You know that."

"Might not be your doing," Jock admitted, "but then there's the other reason."

"What's that?"

"You spent last night with Darlene, from the saloon, right?"

"Part of it. You afraid Mickey'll find out about that? I wouldn't—"

"It's not Mickey I'm worried about."

"Who, then?"

"Bill Clark."

"The sheriff?"

Jock nodded.

"He seems to think he's got a claim on Darlene."

"She's a working girl, Jock, how much of a claim can he have on her?"

"Nevertheless, he wouldn't take too kindly to knowing that you and her spent the night together —with no money changing hands. What she does for money is one thing, but what she does for pleasure is another entirely."

"I see. Are you telling me not to see her anymore while I'm here?"

"There's other girls at the saloon, and Lord knows you'd have no trouble attracting them, but no, that ain't what I'm telling you. I'm just warning you to be careful, is all. I don't have any right to say anything else."

"I appreciate the warning."

"That done, then, let's get these cups washed and go and talk to the sheriff."

"Right."

NINETEEN

On the way to the sheriff's office Clint wanted to stop off at the telegraph office to let Rick Hartman know that he had reached Jericho Flats.

"Yeah, and I've got to check for answers on my telegrams," Jock said.

When they arrived the clerk told Jock there were no replies as yet, and then took Clint's message down and sent it along.

That done, they continued on to the sheriff's office.

Clint had seen Sheriff Bill Clark around town during his other visits to town. Since most of the time he'd spent in Jericho Flats had been spent at the game, in Jock Reynold's livery stable, the two had barely exchanged half a dozen words over the past five years. Actually, Clint did not remember the man as a deputy, but did recall that he had been elected sheriff about three years ago.

They entered the sheriff's office and found Bill Clark seated behind his desk, looking over some posters.

"Good morning, Bill."

Clark looked up and said, "Hello, Jock." His face did not betray his feelings at being interrupted. It was obvious that Jock was not considered a friend, but simply one of the townspeople.

Idly, Clint wondered if Jock sat on the town council.

"Bill, I'd like to introduce you to a friend of mine. This is Clint Adams."

Clark stood up and said, "I'm well aware of who Mr. Adams is, Jock. I've seen him here in the past, though we've never spoken. A pleasure to meet you," Clark said, but he made no attempt to shake hands.

"Sheriff."

"Bill, we've got something we'd like to talk to you about."

"Have a seat, then," Clark said, sitting back down himself.

Jock pulled a chair over, but Clint remained standing.

Carefully, Jock explained the situation to Sheriff Bill Clark, who appeared to listen intently. He was in his early thirties, strong-jawed, with a prominent nose and close-set eyes. Seated, you would think that he was taller than he was. His torso was long and muscular, but his legs did not quite match, so in actuality he was probably about five ten.

"That's the story, Bill. I'm afraid we're expecting a little trouble in the near future."

"Or not-so-near future, if your story is to be believed."

"Believed?"

"Oh, I don't mean to imply that you're lying, but your logic may be wrong. You may just be taking a few coincidences and stringing them together to make something out of nothing. Isn't that possible?"

"Anything's possible, Sheriff," Clint said, speaking for the first time, "but it's highly unlikely that these men just all happened to have been killed months apart, with nothing connecting their murders."

"I guess I am just not as readily anxious to accept that as you and Jock are, Mr. Adams. Still, I appreciate you coming in to keep me informed. I'll certainly keep my eye out for trouble."

He looked down at the posters on his desk again, and it was obvious to Clint that they had been dismissed.

"Sheriff—" Jock began, but Clint put a hand on his shoulder to stop him, and the two men left.

"I don't understand it," Jock said. "He didn't believe a word."

"He's just not as close to it as we are, Jock. We did our job, though. We let him know that trouble might be coming. The rest is up to him."

"He didn't seem a bit friendly, did he?"

"I thought maybe that was just his way."

"He's usually a bit warmer than that. I can't figure—hey, do you think he knows about you and Darlene, already?"

"It's possible, I guess," Clint said. "It might explain his coldness. I'll ask her."

"Won't make your stay here real pleasant if the sheriff's got it in for you."

"That's all right," Clint said. "I'm sure Darlene can more than make up for that."

"Still intend to see her, then?"

"If she's willing."

"Why don't you try one of those other gals? They're all pretty."

"They are that, but Darlene is a little more pretty, don't you think, Jock?"

"I guess so. Listen, I've got some work to do."

"I guess I could find something to do, as well. See you later?"

"Come by the house for dinner."

"Maybe I should tag along—"

"I don't need a baby-sitter, Clint. I'll see you later for dinner."

"All right, Jock. Whatever you say."

Clint decided to go over to Darlene's now and see if she was awake. Might as well find out right off what her relationship with the sheriff was. If it was too much trouble to keep seeing her, there was always one of the other girls in the saloon.

He climbed the stairs on the side of the building and knocked on her door. After a few moments it opened, and she stood there looking tousled and lovely, lips slightly swollen, her dressing gown held tightly around her, emphasizing the full thrust of her breasts. At that moment, there were no other women in town, as far as Clint was concerned.

"Good morning," she said, reaching for his hand. "Come inside."

As soon as she had closed the door behind them she went into his arms and kissed him. He smelled her morning breath, but did not find it unpleasant. Her tongue crept past his teeth, starting a swelling in his groin.

"Glad to see me, I see," she said, pressing up against him.

"Great way to start the morning," he said, sliding his hands behind her to cup her buttocks.

"I know a better way . . ."

After they had made love they lay together on the bed, naked, the breeze from a slightly ajar window cooling the sweat on their bodies. Her nipples reacted, tightening in response to the chill.

Early in the morning, without makeup, she looked

a little older to him than she had the night before. He guessed her as being in her mid-twenties then, but realized now that she might have been just to the far side of thirty. Either way, she was experienced which, if he were to list his criteria for women from one to five, would be at the top of the list. Young women were nice. They were eager, sweet, more susceptible to words, but when it came right down to it, you couldn't beat experience—and he didn't just mean with sex.

"I came here this morning to ask you a question," he said, turning one of her nipples this way and that with his fingers. It was as hard as a little pebble.

"What?" she asked, eyes closed.

"About you and the sheriff."

"Bill Clark?" she asked, opening her eyes. "What about him?"

"Well, I've been advised—warned really—by a friend that he regards you as staked-out territory."

"He may," she admitted, "but I sure don't. Bill Clark and I have been together on occasion, Clint, but I certainly don't feel any sort of . . . obligation to him, any more than I do to you."

The words might have stung him, but he knew better than to take offense. She was speaking the truth. They had met the night before. To think that some sort of a bond had formed between them already would be silly.

"I like him fine," Darlene continued, "but I don't belong to him. Is that what you were worried about?"

"Not worried, really," he said. "I just wanted to clear the air."

"Well," she said, turning toward him, seeking the warmth of his body with her breasts, "consider it cleared."

He put his arm around her to allow her to snuggle closer, and said, "It's clear as a bell."

She didn't hear him, though.

She had fallen asleep.

TWENTY

Later, after they had both awakened and gone their separate ways with no obligation at all to meet later—though they both knew they would—Clint decided to take a turn around the town.

He'd been to Jericho Flats almost a dozen times in the past, but still did not know much more of the town than its main street, the hotel, the saloon, and Jock's livery.

He found a town that was very satisfied with itself as it was. The people were happy, friendly, exchanging greetings with each other and with him. What conversations he heard had nothing whatsoever to do with wishes for growth. The people were simply happy with things the way they were. The town was manageable, and again Clint realized that this was why Jock had chosen it.

Jock was a paradox. Ostensibly the town's blacksmith and livery owner, Clint had rarely seen any horses in his stable other than the ones owned by the players in the game. Clint decided to check and see if there was another livery in town, and found one at the opposite end of town from Jock's that appeared to be doing a lively business.

Where did Jock's money come from, then? Even if his livery were a successful one it still wouldn't generate the amount of cash he obviously had at his command, not in a town this size.

It was probably not any of his business—as Jock had indicated the night before—but Clint couldn't help but be curious. Maybe he'd be able to find out without asking Jock straight out. Maybe if he simply kept his eyes open for the next few days—or weeks—he'd see something that would explain it.

Clint decided to stop at the telegraph office and check for replies.

"Was just gonna send someone to find you or Jock," the clerk said as he walked in.

'Why?"

"Got some answers for you. One from Denver, and one from Dodge City."

Talbot Roper and Bat Masterson!

"Let me see them!"

"Well, they're actually for Jock. I got one here from Texas for you."

"Let me see that one."

As it turned out, Rick's explained what the other two were about.

Bat Masterson had been ambushed just outside of Dodge City, and lay near death with a bullet in his back.

Similarly, Talbot Roper had been attacked in Denver. He'd been stabbed and was in a Denver hospital, recuperating.

"Damn!" he swore. He looked at the clerk and said, "Hand over those others!"

There might be additional information in Jock's replies about his friend, and he wanted to see them.

"Yes, sir!" the clerk said, giving them over.

Clint first read the one from Dodge. It was from Bill Tilghman, who said that Bat's condition was improving, but that because of Clint's earlier telegram they had allowed the general public to think he was dead.

Good thinking, Clint thought. The Killer would

have gone on his way, thinking he'd killed Bat. That would allow him to make his way to Jericho Flats, eventually.

Tilghman finished by saying that he wished he could leave Dodge to hunt the Killer down, but that they had no leads. Clint sent a message telling Tilghman not to worry. The Killer would not be getting away.

Next Clint read the telegram from Denver. It was from Tal Roper himself, dictated from his hospital bed. He'd been set upon by street thugs who had been hired as a diversion, and during the melee the real killer had crept up on him with a knife. As a result of Clint's earlier telegram—Roper had realized what was happening at the last moment and had turned in time to take the knife to the hilt—but in a non-vital spot. He had drawn his gun, then, and chased off the Killer. He did not, however, get a good look at the man.

Clint sent a message back telling Roper to take his time recuperating. He went on to say that he felt sure that the Killer would be coming his way, and he was waiting for him.

"I'll take these to Jock," he told the clerk.

"Yes, sir," the clerk said, still frightened by Clint's outburst of anger.

"Oh, for Christ's sake," Clint said, and tossed the man enough money to ease his fears.

"Thank you, sir."

"Don't mention it!"

Clint went to the livery to find Jock, and when he didn't see him there he went into his office to wait for him. It occurred to him that Jock might be next door, in the house, but the truth of the matter was he was curious about the man's office, which he had only been in twice—once before this trip, and once last night. He had no time to look around, however, as Jock came in moments later.

"What are you doing?" Jock asked, and Clint thought he detected some tension in the man's tone.

"Waiting for you."

"What for?"

Clint waved the telegram and said, "We got some replies."

"From who?"

"Bat Masterson and Talbot Roper."

"Tell me about it," Jock said, sitting at his desk.

Clint related to Jock everything that was contained within the three telegrams, and then told him about the replies he had sent.

"And Bat and Roper will both be all right?"

"That's the impression I get."

"That means the Killer is getting careless, Clint."

"It also means he's after all of us. He'll either go after Luke Short next, or he's on his way here."

"We've got to locate Short."

"We can try, but the Killer went up against better men in Bat and Roper and failed to kill them. Luke is in their class, and the same thing might occur. In fact, Luke might get the Killer, which would save us the trouble."

"Still, we won't know that unless we can locate him."

"I'll go back to the telegraph office, then," Clint said, "and give it a try."

"By the way . . . ," Jock said as Clint was leaving.

"What?"

"Are the dates of the attacks on those telegrams?"

"Oh shit, yeah, let me look," Clint said. "Dodge City on the fifth, and Denver on the seventh —what?" Clint looked at the two pieces of paper again, to be sure he'd read them right.

"That can't be," Jock said, voicing Clint's thoughts. "How could the Killer get from Dodge City to Denver in two days?"

"Well, that's easy," Clint said.

"What?"

"Sure," Clint said. "Jock, we're dealing with two killers here—Jesus, and maybe even more!"

TWENTY-ONE

Clint spent the better part of the afternoon with the telegraph clerk, sending out telegrams in search of Luke Short and, through Rick Hartman, trying to gather the dates that the other men were killed.

That night at dinner, he and Jock went over everything.

"All right," Clint said finally, "judging from the dates I'd say we're dealing with two killers."

Kelly had been killed well before the others, but Jennings and Collins had been done in four days apart, and then Arcel and Ransom about five days apart. With the attempts on Bat and Roper taking place a scant two days apart, it seemed fairly obvious that they were dealing with two men—or women!

"Do you agree?"

"Yes."

"Does that mean that you're looking for two people with a grudge against all of you?"

"No, Mickey," Clint said, "and see if you agree with this, Jock. I think we're dealing with one person who has either hired a killer to help, or has hired two killers to do all the work."

"Makes sense for it to be two hired killers," Jock said. "Whoever is behind this wouldn't want to show his face. Somebody would recognize him and with the warnings we've sent out, he might not get close enough to do the job. Two strangers would have a better chance."

"I agree. All right, we need somebody with a grudge who has enough money to hire two killers."

"I'm still stuck on somebody with a grudge," Jock said, shaking his head.

"Yeah. As far as I can recall, nobody's ever been kicked out of the game."

"And nobody who isn't prepared to lose a bundle and can handle it is allowed to play."

"What if it's somebody's wife?" Mickey asked.

"What?" Jock said.

"Or girlfriend," Mickey went on, warming to her subject. "What if it's a woman behind the whole thing?"

Jock and Clint exchanged glances.

"If everybody is to be killed, Mickey, that means that some woman has hired someone to kill her husband or lover. Does that make sense?"

She shrugged and said defensively, "I was just making suggestions."

"We appreciate you trying to help, honey," her father said, "but why don't you just make some coffee?"

"The coffee's made," she said stiffly. "I'll go and get it."

"I think we insulted her," Clint said.

"She's too young to know what makes somebody a killer," Jock said with feeling. "More and more I wish you'd left her in Texas—tied up, if you had to."

Clint didn't answer, because he knew Jock didn't mean it—at least, the part about tying her up.

"Jock, have you noticed that most of the people in the game don't have any family?"

"I never did, but now that you mention it, yeah, that's true. Why do you suppose that is?"

"I guess gamblers are loners. They don't have to

justify their habits to anyone. A wife would complain every time he lost, and take part of his money every time he won."

"Then I'm the only one with a family," Jock said, turning to look into the kitchen at Mickey.

"Jock, maybe one of us should stay with her at all times."

"Good idea," Jock said. "I'll keep her with me."

Clint was pleased that Jock had said that. He didn't want his own movement restricted.

"I think I'll go over to the saloon and talk to Captain Jack."

"What about?" Jock asked.

"He owns a saloon and tends bar," Clint said. "He'd know as soon as there was a strange face in town."

"Good thinking."

"I'll recruit the old buzzard to keep a lookout for us."

"And while you're there, say hello to Darlene."

"Oh, sure, Jock. I'll do that for you."

"You'll do it," Jock said as Clint headed for the door, "but not for me."

After Clint had gone, Mickey came back with some coffee for Jock.

"Where's Clint going?"

"To the saloon."

"To see that red-haired woman? The real pretty one?"

"I suppose so."

"Is he in love with her, Pa?"

"No, honey. I don't think Clint Adams will ever fall in love with any woman."

"Why not?"

"Because he likes women and they like him. And because he's a drifter. Of course, he ain't an aimless, shiftless drifter. That's not what I mean, but he does move around an awful lot, and he's pretty set in his ways."

"That don't mean he can't fall in love," Mickey said. "It just means he won't ever get married."

Jock looked at his daughter, who was far from ever being his baby again, and said, "I guess you're right about that, honey. I never thought of it that way."

"I have," she said, and somehow Jock didn't think he'd handled the entire conversation right.

TWENTY-TWO

Captain Jack's was doing a brisk business, but as Clint entered he saw that there was no poker game in progress. Maybe he'd taken all of the players' money last night and they'd decided not to return.

He went to the bar and was met by Captain Jack's broad smile.

"What'll it be?"

"A beer and some help."

"Let me get the beer and then ye can tell me about the help."

Jack got the beer then leaned on the bar and said, "Okay, tell me."

"Strangers, Captain Jack. I need to know when there are strangers in town."

"Well, I guess I can help ye there. First thing a stranger does when he hits town is come here for a drink."

"Any in town now, over the past few days?"

"Let me see," Jack said, surveying the room. "Well, there's one of them fellers ye was playing poker with last night."

"Which one?"

"Well, I know the other three 'cause they're from town, but I don't know the stranger's name—wait a second. I saw him in here before." He squinted, trying to see through the smoke, and then brightened. "There he is, sitting in the corner. He was looking

109

for a poker game before, but there weren't no takers."

"Do you know how long he's been in town?"

"Far as I know, yesterday was the first day."

"Thanks, Captain. What's he drinking?"

"Beer."

"Give me a fresh one for him, will you?"

"Sure thing."

Armed with the fresh beer, Clint crossed the floor to the man's table and set the beer down in front of him.

"Evening," he said.

The man looked up, squinting.

"We played poker last night," Clint said, to refresh the man's memory. His own memory told him that this was the man who had complained that he had to quit with all of his money.

"I remember. You won."

"I did that. Figure I owe you a beer. Mind if I sit?"

"Got any cards?"

"I don't play two-handed."

"Sit," the man said in disgust. "Can't get up a game, might as well get a free beer."

"I don't think we were formerly introduced last night," Clint said. "My name's Clint Adams."

"Farmer, Johnny Farmer."

Farmer picked up the beer and sipped it, showing no inclination for further conversation.

"Passing through?" Clint asked.

"I'm always passing through, friend," Farmer said, watching one of the girls walk past. "I come in, I look for a game, I pass through."

"You don't look like a professional gambler."

Farmer focused his eyes on Clint.

"You mean because I don't wear a black suit—or

any kind of suit? I'm a professional at whatever I do.''

Whatever Farmer's real profession was, Clint hoped he did it better than he played poker, but he refrained from commenting on that out loud.

"What else do you do?"

"Hey," Farmer said, "the price of a beer doesn't buy you my life story, you know. If you want to play cards, I'll play cards, otherwise I'm not really the sociable type."

From the way Farmer was watching the girls in the room, though, Clint felt that under the right circumstances he probably *was* sociable.

"Looks like I wasted a beer," Clint said, pushing his chair back to stand up.

"Looks like you did. Come back when you feel like giving some of my money back."

"I won't give it to you, Farmer," Clint said, "you're going to have to win it back."

"It'll be my pleasure."

It'll be impossible, Clint thought.

Heading back to the bar Clint saw Darlene coming down the steps from upstairs. She saw him, and as he continued to the bar she altered her course to intercept him there.

"Hi," she said.

"Hi. Just the lady I wanted to see."

"That's comforting."

"I need a favor."

"What kind of favor?"

"See that fella I just left sitting over there?"

She sneaked a glance over her shoulder and said, "What about him?"

"His name is Johnny Farmer. I need to know about him."

"Know what about him?"

"Know *all* about him."

"And you want me to—"

"—get one of your girlfriends to be real nice to him. Take him upstairs, make him feel like a big man, get him to talk about himself. Think one of them can handle that?"

"Sure," Darlene said. "That's what they get paid for, isn't it?"

"Oh, she'll get paid."

"Which one?"

Clint watched Farmer through the mirror for a few moments and saw him admiring the plump brunette.

"Who's the little dark-haired girl?"

"That's Hannah. Does he like them on the plump side?"

"I'd say yes. He's been watching her for the past few minutes as if she was a sixteen-ounce piece of meat."

"Well, she weighs more than that, but your point is well taken. I'll talk to her."

"Thanks."

"And then you'll owe me a favor," she said, just before walking away.

As she left and walked over to Hannah the batwing doors opened and admitted Sheriff Bill Clark. For a moment Clint wondered if the lawman had seen him and Darlene together, but he quickly decided that he didn't care.

Clark saw Clint at the bar and walked over.

"Buy you a beer, Sheriff?"

"I buy my own, Adams," the lawman said. Captain Jack put one on the bar for him, but Clint did not see any money change hands.

"Just trying to be friendly, Sheriff."

"Let me fill you in on something, Adams. I know about your reputation."

"Oh? Which reputation is that?"

"You used to be a pretty well known *and* well regarded lawman, until you left it behind you for a reputation as a gunman. 'The Gunsmith', isn't that what they call you? That's a little pretentious, isn't it?"

"You talk more like a schoolteacher than a town sheriff," Clint commented.

"Do all lawmen have to be uneducated?"

"They all have to be educated in many different ways, Clark. Using big words wouldn't be at the top of my list."

"No, but using a gun would be, right?"

"That's right."

"And being a ladies' man? How about that?"

"That's up to the individual."

Clint had a feeling they were going to get right to it, here, but he was sort of disappointed when Clark backed off the subject.

"Just make sure that while you're in my town your gun stays in your holster."

"I'll make a note of it."

Clark took his beer and started across the crowded saloon floor. Clint noticed that not many people made a point of moving out of his way. He had the impression that Clark was not well thought of as a lawman.

He watched as Clark approached Darlene, who had her head together with the chunky Hannah. Clark touched her arm, but she said something to him sharply and then turned her attention to Hannah again. The lawman waited while Darlene finished talking, after which Hannah nodded, looked at Clint, and then looked at Farmer. Hannah said something to Darlene, who shook her head. Hannah again looked from Clint to Farmer, then pouted and nodded her head. She said something to Darlene just before walking away from her toward Farmer.

Now Darlene gave her attention to Clark, who only said a few words before she cut him off and said something sharp. His head jerked back sharply as if she had struck him and then he grabbed her arm. Clint pushed away from the bar, but a hand on his shoulder from behind arrested the movement.

"Leave her be, lad," Captain Jack said. "She can handle herself, and you'd be better off not buttin' heads with the local law."

Clint gave in to the pressure of the captain's hand which, he noted, had more strength than he would have thought.

Captain Jack turned out to be right. Darlene turned her tongue on Clark again, then pulled her arm away and walked away from him. Clark stood there, then slammed his half-filled beer mug down on a table, threw Clint a murderous look, and stalked out of the saloon.

"How do people feel about him, Captain?"

"Can't rightly say. It's not as if he's ever been tested in this town. He's held his own with irate drunks, that's all I can say. Another beer?"

"Yeah, one more."

Clint turned and watched Johnny Farmer's table as Hannah sat down. Farmer's face brightened as she started talking to him, and then he leaned forward and said something to her in a low voice. Clint heard her laughter all the way across the floor, and it sounded artificial. Farmer didn't seem to notice, though. He kept talking, she kept laughing, and then they got up and she led him to the stairs and up to the second floor.

"Hannah says you owe her," Darlene said, coming up next to him. "She was kind of sorry that I was sending her after Farmer, and not you."

"How does she intend to collect?"

"In her own way, I suspect."

"How do you feel about that?"

"Hey," Darlene said, "every man's got to pay the price. When she's done she'll report to you in your hotel room."

"If I didn't know any better I'd say you made some kind of deal with that young lady with me as the price."

"Let's just say she'll be by your room to collect payment."

"And where will you be?"

"Alone in my room, pining."

"Sure. What did our friend the sheriff want?"

"Just to talk."

"You didn't talk with him very long."

"I didn't want to talk about what he wanted to talk about."

"He looked like he got sore."

"I suppose he might have," she said, seemingly unconcerned. "I've got to go to work."

"I'll come by later after I've talked to Hannah."

"I don't think so."

"Why not?"

Smiling impishly Darlene said, "Because I don't think you'll be able to walk."

"Sure," he said as she walked away to work the room.

"She's the best, that one," Captain Jack said. "And she's a nice girl, to boot."

"How about Hannah?"

"Ah, that one," Captain Jack said. "Young and juicy, that one. Right now the men like her, but if she puts on a few more pounds I might have to have a talk with her. Men like 'em plump, but not fat. You plannin' on goin' through all my girls?"

"I hadn't planned it, no," Clint said thoughtfully, "but things don't always go the way we plan them, do they?"

TWENTY-THREE

The Killer of Joe Kelly, Al Collins, Ed Ransom, and—he thought—Bat Masterson—watched Clint Adams leaving the saloon and walking toward his saloon. It would have been easy to kill him right there and then, but his orders were not to make a move until he had help. That help was supposed to come from the man who had killed Jennings, Arcel and—they thought—Talbot Roper. Killer #2 was right then taking care of Luke Short, and would be joining Killer #1 any day now.

The man who was paying both killers seemed to feel that it would take both of them to complete the job in Jericho Flats. Of course, neither killer agreed with that, but they *were* working for the man, so they did as he asked.

Killer #1 held out an imaginary rifle, sighted on the Gunsmith's back, and fired silently.

Clint Adams felt a chill, as if someone had just walked on his grave—or wished him in one.

TWENTY-FOUR

When the knock came at the door it was a forceful one, causing Clint to believe that it might be Jock, or Sheriff Bill Clark. When he opened the door he did not expect to see the dark-haired saloon girl, Hannah.

She must have been all of five foot one, with impressive breasts and hips. She marched past him and he closed the door behind her.

"Hello, Hannah."

He hadn't seen her up this close before and now he was pleasantly surprised to see how pretty she really was. She had a beestung mouth with swollen lips and just the beginnings of a double chin which—at this stage—was not unattractive.

"You're Clint Adams, right?"

"Right."

"I get paid up front."

"I understand," he said, reaching into his pocket.

"No, you don't," she said.

She was wearing a shawl and when she dropped it to the floor he saw that she was still wearing her saloon dress. It was very low cut revealing acres of creamy white flesh. She undid some buttons in the front, so that her full breasts fell free. Her nipples were dark brown—darker than Darlene's—and distended.

"I get paid up front," she said again.

"Now," he said, "I understand."

Clint didn't know it right then, but Jock Reynolds had spoken the truth—in part, at least—to Mickey earlier that night. He did indeed like women, and when a woman like Hannah came to him and offered her wares—her substantial and impressive wares—he was not one to turn them down.

He walked to her and palmed her big breasts. She closed her eyes and he popped her nipples between his fingers.

As he bent to take them in his mouth she backed away and said. "I'm too short. You'll break your neck."

She backed away from him and peeled off her dress, kicking it aside. When she was naked he saw what Captain Jack meant. Her hips were wide, her thighs too full. Her belly was a small roll that, if it got any larger, would start to look fat.

"I know, I know," she said. "I can stand to lose some weight, but I'll think about that tomorrow."

She turned, went to the bed, turned it down and climbed onto it. She sat cross-legged, staring at him, and he suddenly knew what she was waiting for.

While she watched him he undressed. He walked to the bed naked, his erection leading the way, and hung his gunbelt on the bedpost. In a flash she was on him, rolling his swollen penis between her fleshy breasts. The head peeked up at her from between her cleavage and she licked it as she continued to roll him back and forth.

Abruptly she abandoned him and lay back on the bed.

"Now you can have them without breaking your neck."

Lying there she was any man's dream of a voluptuous young woman—she must have been twenty-one or two—all soft curves and hidden places, and between her legs was a mat of dark black hair that almost traveled up her belly.

He got in bed next to her and began to kiss her breasts, sliding his hands over her back and her plump buttocks. She reached between them to hold onto his penis and cup his balls.

"Mmmm," she said as he bit her nipples. He took one breast in each hand and found that they were large enough so that he could run one of her nipples up against the other. She squirmed when he did that, and then he realized that he could take both nipples in his mouth at the same time.

"Oh, God," she said when he demonstrated, "that feels so good! Wait!"

She pushed him away then and kept pushing until he lay down on his back. She raised herself over him and came down hard. He slid into her like he was greased and she squealed and rode him that way for a few minutes. She was incredibly wet and he felt her moistness covering his thighs.

"Okay," she said, leaning over so her breasts were in his face, "bite both of them while I ride you. Come on!"

She started to ride him up and down again and he used his hands to squeeze her breasts together and began to bite and suck both nipples at once.

"That's it," she said. "Oooh, yeah, oh that's it, don't stop . . ."

She was riding him so hard now that it was difficult to keep his mouth in contact with her breasts, but he did the best he could, knowing that the dual sensations were driving her into a frenzy.

Suddenly she stiffened and stopped moving. He thought something was wrong until he looked at her face. Her mouth was open, slack, her eyes closed, like she was waiting . . . and when she came she started moving again, jumping up and down on him, bouncing her breasts off his face and squealing and moaning and then when *he* came he had to hold onto her tightly so she wouldn't bounce completely off him . . .

"Jesus, that was grand!" she said when all of the jumping and moaning had stopped. She was still astride him, his semierect penis still buried deeply inside her.

"It *was* fine," he admitted a little breathlessly. She was a small package of energy that could probably wear out three men in one night, let alone one.

"Mmm-hmm," she said. She leaned over and kissed him, and he realized that it was the first time they'd kissed. Her lips felt fine, cushiony and moist, and her tongue was alive in his mouth.

"Hannah," he said, trying to pull her away so he could talk, "could we talk about Johnny Farmer?"

She stopped trying to kiss him and sat up straight, staring down at him. He tried looking at her face, was distracted by her breasts, and then tried harder.

"All right, but we're not done, all right?"

"Fine. What about Johnny Farmer?"

"He's in town to do some kind of job."

"What job?"

"He didn't say, but he bragged that it was gonna bring him a lot of money. He said he was gonna take good care of me. God, he was terrible in bed. He just wanted to climb aboard and take care of himself, and he thought he was doing me a favor. The only way he could ever take care of me *would* be with money. Now you . . ."

"What else did he say?" he asked hurriedly.

"That was all. He had a big job coming up real soon."

"He didn't say when?"

"That was funny," she said, "but I had the feeling that he didn't know when. Just soon."

"And that's all?"

"That's all. Now, my payment—"

"I thought I just paid you," he said as her hungry mouth came down on him again.

"Honey," she said up against his lips, "that was just the first installment."

A couple of hours later Clint knocked on Darlene's door. He leaned against the wall while he waited for her to open it, because his legs were very weak.

"Clint!"

He pushed away from the wall and leaned on her. She put one arm around him and they entered the room. She deposited him on the bed and closed her door.

"I came over," he said as she approached the bed, "just to prove that I *could* walk—but would you mind if we just slept?"

TWENTY-FIVE

The next morning, on his way to Jock's house, Clint passed the office of the *Jericho Flats Gazette* and saw a headline pasted in the window: LUKE SHORT KILLED!

He hurried inside and bought a copy, and read it right there.

According to the story Luke Short had been in San Francisco, at the Alhambra Saloon in Portsmouth Square, when he had been fired upon during a poker game. It went on to say that he had been hit three times and killed instantly.

"When did you get this story?" he asked the man behind the counter.

"You'd have to ask Mr. Peterson. He's the editor."

"Where is he?"

"Mr. Peterson!" the boy shouted. "A man is here to see you."

Peterson, a tall, gray-haired man in his fifties, came out, wiping ink from his hands with an already ink-smudged rag.

"You want to see me?"

"Yes. This Luke Short story. When did you get it?"

"I got it yesterday, but I took it from another newspaper, the *San Francisco Register.*"

"Can I see that paper?"

"Sure." The man disappeared, then came back with the San Francisco paper.

"A friend of mine in San Francisco mails it to me. I get a lot of good items out of it. I don't cop them word for word, though. No, sir, I words mine myself—"

The man was still talking but Clint wasn't listening. As far as he could see, the *Register* article said exactly the same thing as the *Gazette*. The date on the California paper, however, was over a week ago.

The exact date of Short's death was not given.

"Can I keep this?"

"Have to charge you—"

"Fine," Clint said, shoving some money at the man.

"Hey, this is too much—" the editor shouted, but Clint was already gone.

He hurried to Jock's house, and when Mickey answered the door he hurried past her to the kitchen and dropped both newspapers in front of Jock.

"What?" Jock said, seeing the headline.

"It says that Luke was killed during a poker game at the Alhambra."

"Then he wasn't killed by one of our two killers?"

"I don't think so. We'd have to find out the exact date, though. I can contact a couple of private detectives I know in San Francisco and find out."

"Well, let's do it."

"I'll do it," Clint said. "You stay here with Mickey."

As he started out Mickey shouted, "What about breakfast?"

"I'll be back!" Clint shouted over his shoulder.

He ran all the way to the telegraph office and got there as the clerk was opening. It was the same man he had frightened the day before.

"I want to send an emergency telegram."

"S-sure," the man said. His hand started to shake and he couldn't get the key in the lock.

"Relax, Mister," Clint said. "We have to get inside before you can do anything."

"Right, right."

Finally the man got the door open and they went inside.

Clint addressed the telegram to Sam Wing and John Chang, a couple of Chinese private detectives he had met a couple of years before while in San Francisco. [2] He asked them to get him all of the particulars on the shooting of Luke Short and get it back to him as soon as possible.

That done, he paid the clerk, giving him some extra for scaring him again, and then walked back to Jock Reynold's house. Jock was finishing the *Register* story.

Clint sat down and accepted gratefully the cup of coffee Mickey handed him.

"You were closer to Short than I was," Jock said, putting the paper down. "I'm sorry."

Clint waved away his condolences.

"I'm closer to Bat, but Luke was a friend. I'm just upset because I can't see it happening the way the paper said. First of all, I don't know a man alive who could outdraw Luke Short and plug him three times without Luke getting off a shot. Second of all, I didn't think Luke was in that part of the country."

"You think the reports in the papers are wrong?"

"I don't know, but my friends in San Francisco will find out," Clint said, touching the newspapers on the table. Almost to himself he said fervently, "I hope they're wrong."

●　　●　　●

[2] The Gunsmith #27: Chinatown Hell and The Gunsmith II #36: Black Pearl Saloon.

It wasn't until late afternoon that a reply came, signed by Sam Wing. It read:

ACCOUNTS TRUE, AS FAR AS THEY GO. YOUR FRIEND SENDS YOU HIS REGARDS. YOU WILL BE HEARING COMPLETE STORY SOON.

SAM WING

He folded it up small and stuck it in his shirt pocket.

"What does that mean?' Jock asked after Clint let him read the reply. " '. . . true as far as they go'? Is it true, or isn't it?"

"I don't understand," Clint said. "There must be some reason Sam Wing is being this cryptic."

"And who is your friend?"

"I haven't got all that many in San Francisco." He took the telegram back from Jock, read it again, and said, "I'm even more confused then before."

"I guess we'll have to operate on the assumption that Short is dead. If the killers think that Masterson and Roper are also dead, then they should be on their way here."

"Unless they go after the ex-players."

"Or have already finished them."

"I think to play it safe we ought to assume that they're on their way here. We should be ready to greet them."

"I wish I had somewhere to send Michelle."

Although it was almost inane to do so now, Clint asked Jock something he had been wondering about for a while, now.

"If she calls herself 'Mickey'," he asked, "why do you keep calling your daughter 'Michelle'?"

"She doesn't prefer 'Mickey,' " Jock said, "she's just under the impression that I always wanted a boy."

"Did you?"

"Doesn't every man want a son?"

Clint thought back to a time when, for a while, there was a possiblity that he actually did father a son. [3]

"I guess so."

"Michelle can shoot," Jock said. "I guess if we're stuck with her we might as well put her to work. I'll take her into my office and give her one of my rifles."

"I've got both Arcel and Ransom's guns," Clint said. "I'll clean them and give her one, maybe the derringer."

"Useless guns."

"Not from close up."

"I guess, but I don't intend to let this killer—or these killers—get close to my daughter."

"Fine, but I'll have her keep the gun anyway."

"All right."

"I'll meet you back here later this evening."

"For dinner?"

"I think I'll start taking my meals elsewhere, Jock. I don't want to be predictable as to where I'll be at breakfast, lunch, and dinner."

"Good thinking. I'll meet you in the livery. You know how to get in."

"Right. See you then."

Clint left Jock's house, tucking the telegram from San Francisco into his shirt pocket. He did have some idea of what it meant, but he decided to keep it to himself for now, in case he was wrong.

He hoped he wasn't.

---

[3] The Gunsmith #41: Hell with a Pistol.

TWENTY-SIX

Clint went back to his hotel to check on Dan Arcel and Ed Ransom's guns and to take inventory of his own.

He had his converted Colt and his rifle and, from his saddlebag, he took the little hideout Colt New Line that had saved his life more times than he could count. He unloaded it, cleaned it thoroughly, then reloaded it and, unbuttoning his shirt, tucked it inside his shirt and down into his pants. That done, he cleaned both the Colt and his rifle, and then went on to the other guns.

It was when he was working on guns like this that he wished that the only kind of "gunsmith" he was known as was a working one. He got genuine enjoyment out of working with guns he knew he'd never ever have occasion to fire.

He took Arcel's derringer first, broke it open, unloaded it and cleaned it, then reloaded it and set it aside. Too bad it wasn't a larger caliber, but he assumed that Arcel must have been proficient enough with it to be satisfied with a .22 caliber.

After that he took Ransom's big Navy Colt and wondered why the man carried such a large gun. He unloaded it and found that Ransom kept an empty chamber under the hammer.

At least, at first glance it looked empty.

Looking again, Clint saw that there was something in the chamber, although it wasn't a bullet. It appeared to be a round cylinder of paper, a small slip that had been shaped to fit the chamber precisely.

He tried to use his little finger to get it and found that he could not. Rummaging through his saddlebags he finally came up with a stub of a pencil that fit the chamber. Using it, he slid the piece of paper free, then unfurled it and read it.

The contents puzzled him, and he frowned and read it again. Could this have been what had been taken from Arcel's wallet, a slip of paper like this? And why would both Ransom and Arcel feel that they had to hide an I.O.U. Granted, the amount owed was fairly huge—and where did Ed Ransom get *that* kind of money—but still, if the borrower had been willing to sign an I.O.U, why did it have to be hidden?

On the other hand, the I.O.U. might have had nothing at all to do with their deaths, and it could have been something else entirely that had been hidden in Arcel's wallet.

Had all the other men had similar I.O.U.'s?

There were two men he could still ask about that, Bat Masterson and Tal Roper.

Clint cleaned the Navy Colt, even though he had no intentions of giving it to Mickey. He'd forgotten that Ransom's gun was so big, and the girl would never be able to handle it. The recoil alone would break her wrist. He decided that he would give her the New Line and keep the derringer for himself.

He put the Navy Colt away, tucked the derringer into his right boot and the I.O.U. into the left one. That done he left his room and headed for the telegraph office.

He'd have to word these telegrams very carefully. Cryptically.

The way the telegram from Sam Wing had been.
And perhaps now he knew why.

Clint went to the telegraph office and fired off the
two telegrams he had in mind. He thought about
sending Sam Wing another one, but if Sam had been
cryptic with his initial response, there wasn't much
they *could* say beyond that. He'd have to wait until
they could correspond in the open.

"No one gets these answers but me, do you understand?" he told the clerk. He knew he was taking un-
fair advantage of the fact that the man seemed to be
afraid of him, but it was necessary.

"Yes, sir," the man said nervously. "Nobody but
you. I understand."

He didn't give the man any money for his trouble,
because that would have softened the effect of his
words. He'd take care of him later.

"I'll be back later," he said. He made it sound like
a threat, and felt silly for it.

He went to Captain Jack's to check in with the old
sailor as to whether there were any other strangers in
town. As he entered he saw Farmer seated at the
same table, playing solitaire.

Captain Jack was behind the bar and grinned as he
approached.

"Beer?"

"Yep."

When the captain came with the mug Clint asked,
"Don't you ever sleep?"

"I get a few hours."

"How about a relief bartender, to give yourself a
break from time to time?"

"I don't need a break from this," Jack said. "This
is when I'm alive, mate, back here—here and on the
water, and Lord knows if I'll ever get on the water
again."

"Why wouldn't you?"

"Takes money to buy a vessel, you know."

"You could hire on with one."

"I've captained my own vessels for many years, lad. I can't remember the last time I hired on as a hand. No, I'll go back when I can afford my own ship—and maybe sooner than anyone would think."

The captain's last words were ominous, but before Clint could ask him to elaborate he went off to take care of another customer.

In the mirror Clint saw Johnny Farmer rise and walk toward him.

"I've got two players for later tonight," Farmer said with preamble. "You interested in giving me a shot at getting my money back?"

Clint turned to look at him and said, "Sure. What time?"

"You can sit in whenever you get here."

"All right. See you then."

Farmer turned without saying anything further and went back to his solitaire game.

Real friendly fellow.

Jack came back and Clint asked, "Seen any other strangers in town?"

"There was another one yesterday, but he left this morning. I seen him ride out."

"Did you get a name?"

"I don't ask for a name before I serve a drink. He was shorter than you, a little older, with a big mustache."

"Description fits a lot of men."

"That it does."

Clint finished his beer and said, "Thanks, Captain Jack. See you later."

"Playing cards with that Farmer fella?"

"Maybe."

"He's a bad one to play with."

"Why?"

"Fancies himself a good player, and he ain't even close."

"That's why people like me make extra money off people like him."

"And people like him get sore."

"I can't go refusing his money when he's so eager to give it to me."

"Suit yerself, lad."

After he left the saloon Clint stopped at the gunsmith shop to pick up extra .22 loads for the derringer.

"Doesn't strike me as your kind of weapon," the gunsmith said.

"It's for a friend."

Clint left, wondering what would have happened if he had picked out a town years ago and opened a gunsmith shop like that one.

TWENTY-SEVEN

He set the New Line and the derringer on the table in front of Jock and Mickey.

"Have you ever fired a gun, Mickey?"

"She's fired my Henry," Jock said, indicating the rifle, which he'd leaned against the wall.

"Never a handgun?"

She shook her head and her father said, "I never was much good with a handgun."

"This one would fit your hand better," Clint said, touching the derringer, "but you would really have to know how to use it for it to be effective. For that reason I'm going to leave you this one." He touched the New Line. "Pick it up."

She obeyed.

"How does it feel?"

"It's light. I thought it would be heavier."

Clint thought that maybe he should have brought along the Navy Colt so she could see the difference.

"Here," he said, taking his modified Colt from his holster, "hold this in your other hand."

She took it.

"See the difference?"

"It's much heavier."

"And if you fired both you would see that it has a bigger kick." He took the Colt back and holstered it. "Put the New Line in your belt."

She did so.

"Wear it like that for a while, and later we'll go in the back and fire it."

"All right."

"Do your chores, honey, but stay close to the house."

She stared at both of them in turn.

"Is it gonna happen soon?"

"We think so," Clint said.

"It'll be all right," Jock said, and she nodded and went to do her chores.

"Mickey?" Clint called as she headed for the door.

"Yes?"

"The gun's not loaded now. I'll come out in a few minutes and we'll load it."

"Okay."

After she left, Clint looked at Jock and said, "Are you all set?"

"I got my Henry. That's all I need."

"I think from here on in, after I finish drilling Mickey with the gun I just gave her, that we should keep some distance between us. We don't want to give anyone a chance to take the both of us together."

"All right. Did you figure anything else out from that telegram?"

"No, it's still a puzzle."

"Too bad."

"I talked to Captain Jack. He said there was one other stranger here yesterday, but he left town this morning."

"We don't have to worry about him, then."

"Well, he could always double back on us, but for now Farmer's the only one in town that we have to watch."

"Where is he?"

"Still at the saloon. He wants me to play poker

with him tonight, and that's probably a good way to keep an eye on him."

"What about me?"

"You just keep an eye on Mickey," Clint said, standing up, "and leave Farmer to me. I'll go out and show her how to fire the gun, now."

"I hope she won't have to use it."

"I would hope none of us would, but I doubt that this thing is going to be resolved so easily—not after all these deaths."

Clint worked with Mickey for about a half hour, showing her how to hold the gun, showing her how to squeeze the trigger and not jerk it. They used a fence post for a target and he set her about ten feet from it. They got to the point where she wasn't missing by all that much.

Clint loaded the gun for the last time and handed it to her.

"Put it away now and don't take it out unless you need it. If you find that you do have to use it, keep firing until it's empty. One shot is bound to find its mark."

"I could practice some more on my own—"

"No more practice, Mickey. Just put it away. Do as I say, all right?"

"All right, Clint."

She tucked it into her belt and said, "I've got to finish my chores."

"Remember what your father said. Stay close to the house at all times."

"Why can't I go with you?"

"Your father wants you with him, Mickey."

"Does that mean that you want me with you, too?"

"No, it doesn't. Look, I'm going to keep my distance from both you and your father, Mickey. I'r hoping that if there is an attempt it will be on me."

"You'll get killed."

"No, I won't—unless I have you with me to worry about. Then I might get killed. Understand?"

"Yes."

"I have to go now—"

"What are you going to do when this is all over?"

"I'm going to leave town and get on with my life."

"Will you come back for the game?"

"Mickey," he said, taking her by the shoulders, "after all this I don't seriously think there will be a game any more, do you?"

"No, of course not. That was silly."

He took his hands away from her shoulders and said, "Go ahead and finish your work. I'll see you . . . later," he said, although he knew he wouldn't. He'd only see her from a distance from now until this whole thing was wrapped up.

"All right," she said, "but be careful."

"Always," he said, chucking her under the chin.

She grinned and went to finish her work. She was cute, and when she got older she'd be a real beauty.

And he'd be a lot older.

TWENTY-EIGHT

When Clint got to the saloon that evening the poker game Johnny Farmer had promised was already in progress. He knew that Farmer had seen him, but instead of walking to the table he went to the bar.

"Beer," he told Captain Jack.

"Comin' up."

"You know the fellas playing cards with Farmer?" he asked when Jack brought the beer.

"Yep, both of them work in town."

"Did they know him before tonight?"

"He was in here all day trying to set up a game for tonight. Them two just happen to be fellas who were interested in playing."

"They any good?"

"He's winnin'," Jack said. "That ought to tell you something."

"Right."

"You gonna play?"

"Soon as I finish my beer."

"He can't keep his eyes off of you."

"Let him wait."

As it turned out, Johnny Farmer had to wait even longer than Clint had intended. At that moment Darlene came down from upstairs and steered directly for Clint.

"Want to pay for it?" she asked, loud enough for

Jack to hear. "It might be a change for you."

Clint knew that she wanted him to go upstairs with her, so he considered her question and then said, "Why not. I'm always looking for new experiences."

Jack looked puzzled, but he certainly couldn't fault Clint for taking Darlene up on her offer. Clint took his beer with him and followed Darlene. Before ascending the step he took a quick look at Farmer, who seemed somewhat annoyed at the turn of events.

In Darlene's room he asked, "Okay, what was that all about?"

"What do you know about Captain Jack and your friend Jock Reynolds?"

Clint shrugged.

"Not a whole lot. They both have businesses in town. Why?"

"I think I found something out today that might interest you."

"What?"

"Jack has an office in the back, and I was walking down the hall when I heard voices. I didn't mean to listen in, but . . ." She shrugged and went on. "It was Captain Jack and your friend Jock."

"So?"

"So . . . I didn't hear the whole conversation, but I heard enough to know one thing."

Clint waited and then said, "I'll bite. What?"

"They're in business together."

"You mean, the livery—"

"No, I mean that your friend owns a piece of this saloon—a big piece."

Clint digested that for a moment.

"Well, it's not unusual that he wouldn't tell me about that. He's kind of close-mouthed about where his money comes from."

"Well, Jock said that he had invested a lot of

money in this place, and wasn't getting enough in return."

"Darlene, did it sound to you like Captain Jack worked for Jock?"

She thought a moment and said, "Well, now that you mention it, yes, it did. It almost sounded like Jock was telling Jack that if he didn't straighten up he'd fire him and replace him."

"Well then, from what you're saying, I'd say that Captain Jack was acting as a front man for Jock, who actually owns the place."

Darlene thought a moment, then nodded vigorously and said, "That sounds right to me, Clint. There's something else you should know, though."

"What?"

"Last month Jock Reynolds was out of town for almost two weeks."

"Last month? When?"

"Beginning of the month."

Clint frowned. He was getting a lot of free information here, and it was all very interesting, but he couldn't help wondering why.

"Why are you telling me all this, Darlene?"

"Because I have the feeling that whatever it is that is keeping you here in town involves Jock and Captain Jack. If that's the case I just think you should know all you can about them."

Just trying to be helpful, Clint thought. Why was he always suspicious of people like that?

"You came here after Captain Jack, didn't you, Darlene?" he asked.

She nodded.

"Captain Jack is the one who hired me."

"How about the other girls?"

"Hannah came after me," she said after a moment, "but the others were here before me."

"Any of them before Jack?"

"I'd have to ask."

"Do me a favor, will you? If any of them did come here before Jack find out from them who they worked for then, and if Captain Jack seemed to know Jock when he first got to town, or if they met while he was here."

"All right. I'll ask them later tonight. Clint, does any of this help you?"

"It certainly tells me a few things I didn't know before," he said, "and that's always more of a help than not. Thanks, Darlene."

"Hey, where are you going?"

"Downstairs," he said with his hand on the doorknob.

"We're supposed to be transacting business up here," she said coyly. "Don't you want to make it look real?"

He turned and looked at her, then took some money out of his pocket and gave it to her.

"No," he said as she started to undress, "the money is just to make it look good to Jack."

"But, don't you want to—"

"Not when money changes hand. Later, at your place, after work."

She stared at him with a befuddled look on her face and said, "You are the strangest man . . ."

"I like you, too. See you later."

He'd meant it when he said he liked her, that's why he was sorry that he had to be suspicious where she was concerned. Still, people with free information were usually out for something for themselves.

Maybe she was different, though.

Sure.

Clint left her room and went back downstairs. He left his empty beer mug on the end of the bar and walked over to the poker game in progress. From the

imbalance in the money split on the table, Clint could
see that Johnny Farmer was indeed winning—and if
it were a higher stakes game, he'd be winning big.

"Mind if I sit in?"

Farmer looked up, but it was one of the other men
who replied.

"Sure, come ahead. New blood might change the
flow of the cards."

Clint smiled and sat down.

That's what he was counting on.

TWENTY-NINE

Killer #2 rode into town after dark, while Clint Adams was taking more of Johnny Farmer's money. He rode directly to the livery stable on the other side of town, forced the door and put his horse up himself. He'd settle with the liveryman in the morning.

His instructions were to go right to the hotel and take a room. He did so, but when he got the key to his room he considered going over to the saloon for a drink after he dropped his gear, even if it was against instructions.

He didn't have to, however, for when he entered his room he saw that lying on his pillow was a bottle of whiskey. With it was a note containing some additional instructions, which he read, smiling.

His employer thought of everything.

He kicked off his boots, hung his gunbelt on the bedpost, and opened the bottle of whiskey.

He toasted the big one, because he knew that now that he was in Jericho Flats he was going to get to face the Gunsmith. When he gunned the "living legend" down his own reputation would be untouchable.

He wondered about Killer #1. He knew about him, but all he knew was that he existed, he didn't know who he was. He hoped that whoever he was he didn't think that *he* was going to get a chance at the Gunsmith.

That pleasure, Killer #2 thought, was going to be all mine—even if he had to take care of Killer #1 to assure himself of it.

THIRTY

Throughout the game—which immediately began going his way—Clint watched Johnny Farmer carefully. He'd never heard of the man, but that didn't mean that he wasn't either good with a gun, or simply willing to kill for hire. After all, all of the murders had been done in a fashion other than face to face.

Clint felt that it was Farmer's own obsession with winning that was making him lose. The man simply wanted it too badly. He bet too big when he had a good hand, forcing everyone out, and he bluffed with nothing, during which everyone stayed in. Not only was Clint making money, but the other two men were slowly winning theirs back. After two hours, Johnny Farmer was the only loser at the table.

And he didn't like that.

"Something's not right here," he complained loudly.

"What do you mean?" one of the other men asked. "How come when you were winning everything was okay?"

Farmer threw the man a deadly look and said, "I'm too good a player to be losing to any of you, let alone all of you."

"Johnny," Clint said, shuffling his cards, "your

problem is that you're not half the player you think you are—and even if you were, you'd lose. You just press to hard.''

"I'm a good poker player, Adams," Farmer insisted, leaning forward.

Dealing out cards Clint asked, "Then how do you explain the fact that you always lose?''

"I don't *always* lose," the man said, ignoring the cards on the table. "Only when I play you."

Clint suddenly realized that the man might actually be trying to pick a fight.

"And what does that mean?''

"That means that somebody at this table is cheating, and since these two were losing before you came, I guess we know who that is, don't we?''

The saloon fell deadly quiet and everyone turned their attention to the table. The word "cheat" usually did that in a saloon.

"Let me get this straight," Clint said slowly. "Did you just call me a cheater?''

"I did."

"Then I think it's time you left, Farmer. Sore losers are not welcome in this game."

The other two men suddenly pushed their chairs back and got away from the table.

"I ain't leaving while all of my money is on the table in front of you, Adams."

"You've got enough in front of you for a meal and a hotel room somewhere—but not in this town, Farmer. Get up and walk out."

"You walk out, and leave the money on the table —or else they'll carry you out."

Clint sighed. He still had the deck of cards in his left hand.

"The amount of money you've lost here isn't worth dying for, Farmer, believe me. Why don't we just wait for the sheriff—"

"I ain't waitin'," Farmer said, shoving back from the table.

If he'd even been slightly handy with a gun the fact that he first had to shove himself away from the table would have cost him his life. Clint, remaining in the same postion, simply drew and fired under the table. He never allowed himself to sit so close to a table that it would hinder him in going for his gun.

The bullet caught Farmer square in the middle of his belly and he folded up, dropping his gun and falling to the floor.

Clint, confused at the turn of events, holstered his gun and looked at the batwing doors as the sheriff came walking in.

"What the hell—" the sheriff said.

"Self defense, Sheriff," Captain Jack shouted from the bar. "The other man called Adams a cheater and drew first."

"Who else was in this game?" the sheriff called out.

Both men stepped forward.

"Is that the way it went?"

"Yes sir," one said.

"That's how it happened," the other man said.

"Was there any cheating?"

"No, sir," the first man said.

"This man was just losing, Sheriff, and he got sore. There wasn't no cheatin' going on."

Clark walked to the wounded man and crouched down to have a look.

"He's alive, but he's gut shot. He's not going to last." He looked at Clint and said, "You like gut-shooting a man and making him wait to die."

"I fired under the table, Sheriff. There wasn't any time to pick a target."

Clark scowled and stood up.

"I want three men to carry this fella over to the doctor's."

Three men stepped forward, and as they were carrying Farmer out through the batwing doors, Jock Reynolds and Mickey pushed past them.

"What happened?" Jock demanded.

"Clint! Are you all right?" Mickey asked.

"I'm fine."

"Your friend just killed a man over a game of poker."

"That's not fair," Darlene said, stepping forward. She gave Clark a belligerent look and said, "Clint didn't have any choice."

"I killed him to keep from being killed myself," Clint told Jock.

"You're sticking up for him, too, huh?" Clark said to Darlene. "A common gunman." He whirled on Clint and said, "I want you out of town—"

"Hold on, Sheriff," Jock said, stepping between Clark and Clint. "I'm a merchant in this town and Clint Adams works with me. There's nothing that took place here that you can run him out of town for."

"I can ask him to leave town."

"And he can refuse, which he does."

Suddenly, Clark realized how unpopular he was making himself. Reynolds, Captain Jack, even Darlene, were all siding with the Gunsmith.

"Stay then and be damned!" he said, and stalked out.

"Would you like a drink?" Darlene asked Clint, putting her hands on his shoulders.

He was still seated and looked up at her.

"I'd like one, yes, and buy a round for the house."

"You heard the man, gents!" Captain Jack bellowed. "Drinks on the house!"

Everyone made a beeline for the bar except for Jock and Mickey.

"Take a seat," Clint told Jock. "You, too, Mickey."

Darlene came back and brought Clint a drink, then put one in front of Jock.

"What would the child like?" Darlene asked with her hand on Clint's shoulder.

"I'm not a child!" Mickey said, glaring at Darlene, trying to wish her hand to fall off at the wrist.

"Bring her a glass of milk," Jock said. "Be quiet, girl!"

Mickey sulked while Darlene went to get her a glass of milk.

"What happened here?" Jock asked.

"I'm confused," Clint said. "I had Farmer pegged as one of the killers, but then he goes and pulls a stunt like this, taking me on face to face."

"So? He lost. Are you complaining."

"It doesn't fit the pattern, Jock," Clint explained. "None of the others were challenged. They were shot from ambush."

"I see what you mean."

"I guess I was wrong," Clint said. "Farmer was a hardcase and a lousy poker player, but he wasn't one of the killers."

"Which puts us back where we were."

"Damn," Clint said, "but he told one of the girls here that he was here for a job, a big money job."

"Must have been something else."

Darlene came back with Mickey's milk and put it in front of her.

"You boys want another drink?"

"No, thanks, Darlene," Clint said, and Jock shook his head. Mickey refused to look at Darlene.

When the girl left Jock looked down at the cards in front of him.

"Was this his hand?"

"Yes."

The face-up card was an ace, and when Jock turned over the two hole cards they were also aces.

"Jesus," Jock said, "this guy was just a loser all the way around, wasn't he?"

THIRTY-ONE

"I don't think that little girl liked me very much," Darlene said to Clint later.

They were in her room and had just finished making love. She was lying with her head on his chest.

"She's fourteen. When you're fourteen you think you're all grown up."

"She also thinks that she's in love with you, doesn't she?"

"Maybe."

"Maybe nothing," Darlene said, lifting her head up to look at him. "That young girl is in love with you, Mr. Adams, whether you want to admit it or not."

"I've got other things to worry about besides a schoolgirl crush," Clint said.

"Don't dismiss her so lightly, Clint."

"I'm not dismissing her, Darlene, I'm just setting her aside for now."

She put her head back down on his chest.

"I heard some of what you and Jock were talking about," she said in a low voice. "You're waiting for a couple of killers to come to town."

"I thought that Johnny Farmer was one of them, but it looks like I was wrong," he said, still puzzled. "Hannah told me that he told her he was here for some big money job. I thought for sure I had him spotted."

"So what do you do now?"

"Wait."

"Wait for two killers to try and kill you? That's crazy, Clint."

"Darlene, these men—and the man they work for—are responsible for the deaths of several of my friends, and have wounded a couple of others. It's not a question of my wanting to wait for them, but better I wait here than I get shot in the back somewhere else. It's not as if I had a choice. One way or another our paths would cross. I'm just trying to make sure that the odds are in my favor when they do."

"Well, I have to say that I've never seen anyone move as fast as you did tonight. In fact, I didn't even see you draw your gun. You're as fast as they say you are."

Clint had no answer for that, so he simply remained silent.

"You don't want to talk about this tonight, do you?" she asked, pushing her nose against his chest.

"No."

He felt her tongue start to travel across his chest, first to one nipple, then the other.

"You want to forget all about what happened tonight, don't you?"

"Yes."

She was tracing a warm, wet path down his chest now, over his belly, working inexorably toward his rapidly burgeoning shaft.

"And you want me to help you, don't you?"

"Yes—Darlene—" he said her name and caught his breath as her mouth came down on him, drawing him in, wetting him, sucking him. She used her hand to pump his shaft while her mouth worked up and down on it, and before long he was exploding, filling her mouth, riding the crest of an incredible wave of pleasure—and yet it was all still there, in the back of his mind, even as he lifted his hips while she drained the last drops from him.

She let him slide from her mouth, but she wasn't done—not by a long shot. She began to suck him again, using her hands to fondle his balls, manipulate his penis, trying to bring him erect again.

He thought about the piece of paper, the I.O.U., he'd found in Ed Ransom's Navy Colt.

Incredibly, she had him erect again and was sucking him eagerly, noisily . . .

He thought of the hidden compartment in Dan Arcel's wallet.

It would take longer this time, because it was so soon after the first time—which was actually the *second* time, wasn't it?—but she didn't seem to mind. She slid her hands beneath him, cupping his buttocks, sucking at him vigorously, anxiously, expertly . . .

What if the same slip of paper had been in Arcel's wallet? And what if Jennings, and Collins, and Kelly also had one?

He felt it building in his legs and reached down to cup her head. She was using long, slow strokes now, moaning, sucking him to the brink of another incredible orgasm . . .

He still had to find out if Bat and Tal Roper had any such papers.

. . . and suddenly she released him. He groaned as she slid up onto him, raising her hips, and impaled herself on him, taking him deep inside her slick, wet warmth. Her mouth came down on his, also wet and warm, eager and hungry . . .

His thoughts came back to the present as it took all of his willpower not to explode right then and there inside of her. She began to ride him, and he had to give her all of his attention. He sucked on her breasts

as she pressed them to his face, and cupped her buttocks, drawing her to him . . .

. . . and for a few moments, he actually did forget
everything else.

Lisa Hardy didn't know who the man was. All she
knew was that Captain Jack had given her the room
number and told her to go over there. He told her to
make sure that the man enjoyed himself, and she had
pouted at him and asked when he ever knew a man to
complain.

Good old Captain Jack. He took care of his girls,
and Lisa was one of his favorites. She visited him in
his room every once in a while, too, just to make sure
she stayed his favorite. The other girls teased her
about that—calling Captain Jack a dried-up old
man—but they didn't know the half of it.

For an old man Captain Jack sure had a big one,
and could last longer than most men half his age.

Killer #2 answered the knock at his door and saw
the girl standing there. Tall and firm, ripe breasts
almost bursting from her low-cut gown.

Yes, sir, his employer sure thought of everything.

THIRTY-TWO

Clint was at the telegraph office as soon as it opened the next morning. The clerk behind the desk groaned when he saw the Gunsmith enter. He'd already heard the stories of how Clint Adams had gunned a man in the saloon the night before. Everyone who was there swore they never saw him draw his gun.

"Uh, 'morning, Mr. Adams."

"Did those replies come in?"

"Late yesterday, while I was closing. I saved them for you, just like you said," the man said, handing them over.

"Thanks."

"You didn't say nothing about finding you when they came in," the man said while Clint eagerly read them, "so I just held them for you, just like you told me to do."

Clint read Bat's reply first, then Roper's. They both said the same thing.

Neither man had an I.O.U.—and that just confused things even more.

"Thanks," he told the man, and left.

He went to a café to have breakfast and think things over. If Bat and Roper had had I.O.U.'s it sure would have made things simpler. In that case, the I.O.U.'s would have been the motive. Everyone holding one would either have been killed, or

wounded in a murder attempt, all of which were
aimed at getting back those I.O.U.'s.

Now, with Bat and Roper not having any, what
was the importance of the I.O.U. he'd found in Ed
Ransom's gun? And the hideout compartment in
Arcel's wallet?

He was going to have to make sure he spoke to
Darlene around midday, because she was supposed
to have talked to the other girls by then about Captain Jack.

When his breakfast came Clint was studying the
I.O.U., and he hastily put it away in his shirt pocket
and began eating.

At midday he knocked on Darlene's door, and she
answered.

"Come on in," she said.

She was dressed, having just gotten there herself
moments before.

"Did you talk to the girls?"

"I did. Hannah told me that when Lisa got here
she worked for a man named Dobins. It was a few
months afterward that Dobins disappeared and Captain Jack was suddenly the owner of the saloon. He
changed the name and added all that stuff on the
walls."

"What do you mean, Dobins disappeared."

"He just wasn't there one day and Captain Jack
was. He told the girls that they were working for
him."

"And they accepted that?"

"He showed them a bill of sale."

"How does Hannah know all of this?"

"She and Lisa are friends."

"What about Captain Jack and Jock?"

"Hannah didn't know."

"How many girls who were here then are still here?"

"One, just Lisa."

"Will she talk to me?"

"I'm sure she will."

"Where is she now?"

"I don't know. She wasn't at the saloon when I went over to talk to the girls. Hannah didn't know where she was, either."

"Let's find her," Clint said. "I want to ask her some questions."

They left together and when they got to the street they saw that there was some commotion at the far end of the block.

"What's happening there?" Darlene asked.

"I don't know. Let's take a look."

They walked that way and Clint began pushing through the crowd with Darlene right behind him.

"Did anyone call the sheriff?" someone asked.

"He's on his way," somebody said.

"What a shame," another voice said.

"What's she doing in there?"

As Clint broke through the crowd he saw what the crowd was talking about. They were gathered around a horse trough and in the water was the body of a young woman.

"Clint—" Darlene said.

He tried to stop her but it was too late. She stepped around him and looked.

"Oh, my God!" she said, her hands flying to her mouth.

"Do you know her, Darlene?"

She nodded, her eyes wide with shock.

"Yes," she said. "Clint . . . that's Lisa!"

THIRTY-THREE

"What's your interest, Adams?" the sheriff demanded.

"I wanted to talk to the girl today, Sheriff, and now she's dead. I want to know how and why!"

They were at the undertaker's office. The girl's body had finally been removed from the water and laid out in the undertaker's back room where the doctor could examine her body to determine how she died.

"This isn't any of your business, Adams."

"I'm making it my business."

Clint had taken Darlene back to her room, where she was lying down. Hannah and the other girls—not to mention Captain Jack—must have heard the news by now.

"If you do you're stepping over the line, Mr. Gunsmith. I can run you out of town for interfering—"

"Cut the crap, Clark. If anything I'm trying to help you, too."

"Can you two keep it down?" the doctor said, coming through the curtained doorway from the back room. "You'll wake that poor girl up."

"She's dead, Doc!" Clark said.

"I know."

Both men fell silent then, waiting for the doctor's report.

"Well, I hate to say this, but that girl drowned to death."

"What?" Clark asked.

"Someone drowned her in that trough. An ugly way to die."

"There's no pretty way, Doc," Clint said.

The doctor examined Clint for a minute and then said, "You look like a young man who would know that." The physician was certainly old enough to refer to Clint as a "young man."

"Doc . . ." Clark said, looking confused, "nobody heard her?"

"It probably happened late last night, and if the man was strong enough it could have been done silently."

"Jesus," Clark said.

"Doc, you'd better check on the girls at the saloon," Clint said. "Some of them might need something to calm them down."

"I'll go over there right now." He looked behind him at the doorway and said, "Terrible thing. She must have been very pretty."

Clint felt ashamed, somehow, that he couldn't comment on that. He honestly didn't remember the girl.

"Can I get started, Sheriff?" the undertaker asked. He was a roly-poly man in his forties, and Clint was glad to see for once an undertaker who was *not* cadaverous looking himself.

"Huh—oh yeah, sure, Willy."

"Will you check and see if she had any family?"

"Yeah, I'll do that."

The sheriff walked to the door to leave and Clint followed him.

"Adams—" he said angrily outside, when he realized that Clint was with him.

"Sheriff, answer me one question."

"What?"

"Are you equipped to deal with this?"

An angry retort was almost past his lips when the lawman bit it back.

"No," he admitted tightly.

"I can help you, then. I've dealt with this kind of thing before."

"How do I know you didn't kill her?"

"Because I'm telling you I didn't."

"Where were you last night?"

"I wasn't alone, if that's what you want to know."

"Can you prove it?"

"Yes, if you force me to, but you might not like the answer."

Clark knew what he meant and tightened his jaw.

"Now I'm offering you my help. Let's just find out who killed the girl without fighting about it."

Sheriff Clark thought it over for a few moments, then nodded and said, "All right, then. What do you suggest?"

"Question Captain Jack. See if he had Lisa visiting anyone last night, after hours. If not, check with the girls, see if she wasn't seeing someone on the side. Also, ask them if she has family you could notify."

"What are you going to do?"

"I'm going to ask questions of people who live on the street where that trough is, see if anyone heard anything. We'll meet at your office in about an hour. All right?"

"Agreed."

Without further word the sheriff started for the saloon.

Somehow, Clint knew that Lisa Hardy's death had

something to do with the reason he was in Jericho
Flats. It was too much of a coincidence that she
would turn up dead on the day he needed her to
answer some questions.

About Captain Jack.

THIRTY-FOUR

The sheriff was already in his office when Clint got there. The interviews must not have taken long. Clint said as much.

"It doesn't take very long for poeple to tell you that they don't know anything."

"Not even Captain Jack?"

"He said that as far as he knew all his girls were in bed—alone."

"And her friend, Hannah?"

"The plump little one?" Clark asked. "She claimed that Lisa Hardy wasn't seeing anyone secretly."

"Well, she sneaked out to see *somebody*, or she wouldn't be dead."

"What did you get?"

"Nothing. Nobody heard anything—or if they did, they're not saying."

"Where does that leave us?"

"In the dark—for now."

"You've got some ideas?"

"Not really," Clint lied. He did have some ideas, but none that he wanted to share with the sheriff.

"Well, then, I guess this partnership hasn't accomplished very much."

"Let's not dissolve it just yet, Sheriff," Clint suggested. "We're all we've got."

"What do you suggest, then?"

"Just have your deputies go around talking to people. Maybe somebody from another part of town was passing by and heard or saw something."

"What are you going to be doing?"

"I think I'll talk to Hannah again. She and the dead girl were good friends. She must know something."

Clint found Hannah in her room at the saloon, crying. A couple of the girls were with her, trying to comfort her. Darlene was one of them.

"Do you have to talk to her now?" Darlene asked.

"She's got to know something she's not telling, Darlene."

"Like what?"

"Whatever it is, she has to understand that she can't get Lisa in trouble now."

"Let me talk to her," Darlene said. "Wait out in the hall."

"All right."

Clint waited outside for fifteen minutes, and then Darlene came out.

"All right, she'll talk to you."

Clint went in and the other girl left. Hannah reached for Darlene's hand.

"Will you stay with me?"

"Sure, hon."

"Hannah, you knew Lisa was going to sneak out last night, didn't you?"

"She didn't."

"She must have—"

"She didn't sneak," Hannah said. "Captain Jack sent her to the hotel."

"Jack?"

"She said he had somebody he wanted her to treat real special."

"Jack told the sheriff he didn't know why she was

out," Clint said to Darlene.

"Then he lied," she said.

"Are you sure about this, Hannah?"

"Yes."

"How can you be so sure?"

"Because Jack asked me to go over first, but I didn't want to. Some of his friends are . . .weird."

"Why would Lisa agree, then?"

"She thought she was Jack's favorite, and she wanted to stay his favorite."

So she went and never came back. Did that mean that the man she went to see killed her, or that she was simply killed by someone on the way back?

"All right, Hannah. Thank you."

"It doesn't matter if you find the man who did it," Hannah said. "It won't bring her back."

"I know," Clint said, "but I have to try, anyway."

He nodded to Darlene, and left.

Captain Jack was nowhere to be found in the saloon—not even in his office—so Clint went to the hotel next, to talk to the hotel clerk.

"I saw her come in," the clerk admitted, "but I didn't see her go out."

"Do you know what room she went to?"

The man shrugged and said, "For all I know she could have gone to yours."

"Did anyone check in yesterday?"

"One man," the clerk said, and then he shuddered and said, "mean-looking. In fact, he checked in after dark."

"What's his name?"

The clerk squinted at the registered and said, "Jack Smith."

"Smith," Clint repeated. Whatever happened to "John?" "What room?"

"Eighteen."

"Thanks."

Clint started for the steps but the clerk said, "He ain't up there now."

"Where is he?"

"I don't know where he is, I just know where he ain't—and he ain't in his room."

"How do you know?"

"I seen him go out earlier."

"Is there a back way to this hotel?"

"Sure."

"Then he could have taken the girl out that way last night, and then come back in?"

"Sure," the clerk said again.

"All right. Thanks."

Clint left the hotel, wondering what his next move should be. He wanted to talk to the stranger, or to Captain Jack, but since he couldn't find Captain Jack, the wise move would probably be to talk to the next best person.

His apparent partner.

Jock Reynolds.

THIRTY-FIVE

Clint went to Jock's house and found Mickey there
. . . alone.

"Where's your father?"

"He had to go out.'

"We agreed that he would stay with you all the
time."

She shrugged and said, "Captain Jack came over
here in a big hurry this morning, and Pa said he had
to leave. He told me to stay inside."

"How long has your father known Captain Jack,
Mickey?"

"I don't know."

"Have they spent a lot of time together since Jack
arrived in town?"

"I've seen them together sometimes, but not really
a lot. Why?"

"Never mind. Stay put, I'm going to try and find
your father."

"What's happened? There was a big crowd down
the street this morning."

"I'll tell you later. Right now I want to find your
father and talk to him."

"Clint, you're scaring me," she said. She took the
New Line out of her belt.

"Good." He pointed to the door. "Anybody
comes through that door, you pull the trigger until
that gun is empty."

She started to protest, but Clint left and headed for Jock's livery.

The front doors were locked again, so he went around the side and used the key to get in. It was dark, and he lit a match so he could see where he was going. There were several horses inside—including Duke—but the dark didn't seem to be bothering them.

He made his way to Jock's office and lit a storm lamp he found there. He looked up at the wall. Jock's Henry was missing, but the Winchester and the Sharps were still there. Big gun, the Sharps. Big enough to punch a man's chest from three hundred yards or more.

Like Dan Arcel.

If Jock owned such a gun, it was a good bet he knew how to use it.

Clint sat at Jock's desk and idly began looking at the papers on top. After that he started opening and closing drawers. Before long he had launched a full-scale search of the desk, not knowing what he was looking for—but knowing it when he found it.

It was in a very small drawer that you could very easily miss if you weren't searching. One piece of paper, and then several pieces of paper. Clint spread them all out on the desktop, then took the one he had taken from Ed Ransom's gun and spread that one out, too.

Five of them, five I.O.U.'s, made out to Joe Kelly, Dave Jennings, All Collings, Dan Arcel, and Ed Ransom.

All for considerable sums of money, and all signed by the same man, who was in debt to all of these men.

Jock Reynolds.

He heard a noise behind him, but he was too late. He'd been so intent in his search that he hadn't heard them when they first entered, and now it was too late.

He turned slowly and saw the three of them: Captain Jack, a stranger—probably the man from the hotel—and Jock Reynolds.

They all held guns, and they were all pointed at him.

"You put the pieces of the puzzle together, Clint?" Jock asked.

"I think so, Jock."

"That's good. My puzzle just fell into place, too, and you're the final piece."

THIRTY-SIX

Clint sat there staring at the three men.

"You forget that Bat and Tal Roper are still alive," Clint said.

"It doesn't matter anyway," Jock said. "They won't know what happened."

"You owed these five men money, and decided to kill them rather than pay off."

"Paying them all off would have put me out of business," Jock said, "and all of a sudden they all wanted to be paid off at the same time."

"You tried to kill Bat and Roper and Luke Short, just as a blind, so nobody would think that it was only these five men who were targets."

"Just in case the I.O.U.'s came to light, I didn't want them to stand out as a motive."

"Where does Captain Jack enter into all of this?"

"Jack is just a business partner. I have a lot of business partners all over the country, Clint. You once asked me where my money came from. Are you still curious?"

"Of course." He'd be as curious as he had to be to keep himself alive a little longer.

"Jack, get Clint's gun."

Captain Jack came forward and gingerly removed the Gunsmith's modified Colt from his holster.

"Check his boot. There's got to be a derringer someplace."

Jack put his hand inside Clint's boot and found the derringer, showing it to Jock.

"Not my kind of weapon anyway," Clint said with a shrug.

Jack went back to his place next to Jock, who started talking.

"I used to be in another business, Clint, many years ago. I stole. I stole from banks and stages and trains, and I wasn't fancy like most of them. I kept a low profile. Nobody knew my name, I didn't have a reputation to live down when I retired."

"And you retired to here."

"I opened this business just as a front, and also bought out the owner of the saloon."

"Dobins?"

"You heard about him?"

"I heard he disappeared."

"Well, he didn't really want to sell, so I persuaded him."

"And then Captain Jack became your front man."

"Jack's really not an ex-sailor. Oh, he always wanted to be a sailor, but he used to ride with me in the old days."

"And this fella? I presume this is 'Jack Smith', who registered at the hotel last night."

"Jack Smith," Jock said with a grimace. "His real name is Joshua Grimes, and although he doesn't have a lot of imagination, he's very good with a gun."

"He's also good at killing women, I presume."

"That was my idea. When I heard that you were asking questions, I knew that she was the only one who might give Jack and me away."

"It was a mistake, Jock."

"I admit that, but then I didn't expect Grimes to drown her in the horse trough and leave her there, causing an uproar in town."

"I thought you said he was good."

"He is, but he used poor judgment in this case."

"Good enough to kill a man with your Sharps at over three hundred yards, with one shot?"

"I don't know if he's that good."

"Arcel knows."

"I did Arcel, Clint. He was the only one I did myself. I hired Farmer and Grimes—both of whom also used to ride with me—to do the rest."

"Farmer was your man, then?"

"Yeah. He was good enough to handle Ransom and Jennings, but he got greedy. He thought if he shot you down after calling you a card cheat he'd have a big reputation. See, Grimes and Farmer never took to retirement like Jack and I did. Grimes went on to become a fairly successful gun for hire, and Farmer—well, he was not as successful."

"I can see why."

"Yes, but Grimes, on the other hand, he's very good."

"You keep saying that. Are we going to get a chance to find out how good?"

"I don't think so."

"Jock—" Grimes said.

"I really don't think Grimes is quite ready for you, Clint."

"Jock, you promised—" Grimes said.

"I promised you that you could kill him," Jock said, "and you can—but I'm not going to take a chance on him outgunning you on the street. I can't take that risk, Grimes."

"Well, I get to kill him, anyway. At least I'll be known as the man who killed him. Nobody has to know how."

"Right."

"I don't get it, Jock," Clint said. "If you retired with so much money, why did you have to borrow from these men? And where did they get so much money to loan you?"

"It wasn't a loan, really, it was an investment. I had big ideas, Clint, some of which paid off. I own four successful gambling houses, as well as the saloon here, and they're all run the same way, with front men."

"Still keeping a low profile, huh?"

"That's right."

"And paying them off would put you out of business? I can't believe that. If you're as successful as you claim there's not that much money involved."

"Well, I think they compared notes and decided that it would be fun for all of them to demand their money back at one time."

"I guess your successes with their money didn't sit well with them."

"I don't see why not. I would have paid them off eventually."

"I don't believe that for a minute."

"No," Jock said after a moment, "neither do I. Paying them wouldn't have broke me, but the bastards were charging me interest. I just couldn't bring myself to part with all that money."

"So you devised a plan to kill them, but to add other deaths as well as a blind. You picked the other players in the game."

"I thought that had a certain flair."

"You picked your friends, Jock?"

"Oh, come on, Clint. None of us were friends. We met twice a year to try and take each other's money. That certainly didn't make us friends."

"Well, that doesn't explain where they got the money to give you."

"How can you have the reputation you do and be so naive? Jennings and Collins sat on the town councils in their respective towns. They skimmed money right and left and built themselves a tidy bankroll. Arcel played in a lot of high stakes games, and he was good. Ransom cheated his company, and how they never caught on I'll never know."

"And what about Joe Kelly? He was a United States marshal."

"And as crooked as they come," Jock said. "He raked it in with both hands, Clint, like you could have done if you were as smart as he was."

"What was the idea of dumping him in the whorehouse?"

"That was Grimes here. He has a warped sense of humor. Kelly had arrested him once, and Grimes wanted to settle the score. He knew Kelly was married, so he dropped him off in the whorehouse after he killed him."

Clint looked at Grimes speculatively. If he got the drop on Kelly, then he was better than Jock gave him credit for.

"Does that wrap it all up for you?" Jock asked.

"All but one thing."

He looked past Jock at something he'd never noticed before. There was a window between the office and the livery. He memorized its location.

"What's that?"

"Why did you send Mickey to get me?"

"I didn't send here to *get* you," he said. "That was her own idea. I sent her to *stay* with you, just in case Grimes or Farmer missed and somebody came looking for me."

"They *did* miss."

"I can't fault them for that. Bat Masterson and Talbot Roper are nothing to sneeze at, but it turned out okay. Masterson and Roper will rest easy knowing that you're here, and by the time they find out that you're dead, it'll be too late for them to do anything."

"Which one of your bright boys killed Luke Short?"

Jock looked at Grimes.

"It wasn't me," the gunman said. "I wish it was, but I couldn't find the bastard."

"Well, it couldn't have been Farmer. He wasn't good enough."

"Well, if Grimes didn't do it," Clint said, "and Farmer didn't do it, who did?"

No one had an answer, but Clint thought he did. As the others were groping for one, the side door suddenly opened, lighting the interior a bit.

"Pa!" Mickey's voice called out.

"Michelle, get back to the house!" Jock shouted. He turned, and Jack also looked. Since both of them were looking, it was inevitable that Grimes's eyes would flick that way, just for a second . . .

"Mickey, run!" Clint shouted.

He leaped for the light and knocked it off the desk. It fell to the floor and extinguished without starting a fire. That was too bad. A blaze might have worked in his favor.

In the dark he lunged for the Winchester in the wall, the location of which he'd memorized. His hand close on it and he jerked it off and threw himself to the floor just as several shots rang out.

There was that window between Jock's office and the livery. Clint had memorized its location as well, and now he flung himself at it, hoping he would not be off and hit the wall.

He didn't.

The sound of breaking glass was tremendous in the enclosed space, and Clint felt shards tear at his face and he fell through it.

THIRTY-SEVEN

It was pitch-dark in the livery.

Somebody could have moved for the door, but as soon as it opened Clint intended to open fire. He only hoped that Mickey wouldn't come back.

He felt blood trickling down his face from two places, a gash on his left cheek—great, another scar—and a cut in his right eyebrow. He sat with his back against the side of a stall, waiting and listening.

After he had crashed through the glass there had been a lot of commotion and shouting. Mostly Jock shouted at Grimes and Jack, who were stumbling around in the dark in the small office. Jock wanted them to stay still and keep quiet. Eventually, he managed to get them to obey.

Now they were all just waiting and listening, hoping that the other would give himself away.

Clint heard somebody move and groan, and guessed that it would be "Captain" Jack. The old man's knees and legs were probably bothering him, and he was trying to stretch some life into them.

A few minutes later Clint heard Duke move in his stall, and that's when he knew he was going to have to make the first move. Jock was too smart not to figure out that he could threaten Duke's welfare, or he might even try to kill the big horse out of spite.

"Jock, let's talk about this," he said aloud.

"About what, Clint?"

"We can make a deal."

"You want to deal?" Jock asked. The disbelief was plain in his tone of voice. "I could believe that if you were Joe Kelly, Clint, but I know you better than that. You'd never go for a deal. After all, we killed your friend, Luke Short, and we tried to kill Masterson and Roper, also your friends. I know you well enough to know that you don't take that sort of thing lightly."

"I'm not alone, Jock."

There was a new kind of silence then, and Jock asked, "What the hell does that mean?"

"Think about it. Grimes didn't kill Luke Short, and I know damned well Farmer couldn't have done it. What does that tell you?"

He heard a muttered "damn" and then Jock said, "Short's alive?"

"And in town. We set this up together. We faked his death, and then he rode here to help me. See, I knew about you all along."

Jock laughed.

"You had me going there for a moment, Clint, but you pushed too hard. You didn't know anything until you found those I.O.U.'s."

"You're wrong, Jock. I knew when I found Ed Ransom's hidden I.O.U., the one your boy missed finding."

"You're a dead man, Clint," Jock said.

All three of them began to fire at the sound of his voice, and Clint scooted out of position quickly, moving into an empty stall.

"Grimes! Jack!" Jock shouted. "He's got to be in front of us. We'll work our way toward the front until we pin him to the wall. Then he's ours."

In the dark Clint didn't know which way to go. He'd memorized the position of the rifle, and the window and side door, but not much beyond that.

Jock, on the other hand, owned the place. He knew every inch of it.

Clint knew he was in trouble.

All of a sudden they all heard the tremendous boom of a shotgun, both barrels. It sounded like it came from the front of the livery, outside. Suddenly, the front doors began to swing open, bathing the interior in bright light.

Clint didn't have time to see who it was. Captain Jack was right across from him and they saw each other at the same time. Jack tried to bring Clint's own gun to bear on him, but Clint pulled the trigger of the Winchester. The slug hit Jack in the forehead and took most of the back of his head with it as it went straight through.

Clint scrambled over to the body and grabbed his gun from Jack's limp hand.

He saw Grimes then, in a corner, but the gunman had already seen him. Clint knew he'd never make it. Grimes was about to pull the trigger when there was another shot. Grimes grunted as a slug plowed into his chest, and he fell forward onto his face.

Clint turned and saw Luke Short standing there, his gun in his hand.

"Thanks."

"You're welcome."

"But what took you so long?" he demanded.

Short, a short, slender, well-dressed man with a carefully-cared-for mustache, gave Clint a look and said, "Don't tell me you expected me?"

"Of course I did," Clint said, standing up.

"Did not," Short said.

"Yes, I did."

"Did not."

"Could we discuss this another time? There's one more man, you know."

"Where?"

Clint looked around and saw that the side door was now open.

"Come on," he said.

They rushed out the side door and Clint wondered if Jock would make for the house. He wouldn't dare use his own daughter as a shield, would he? Putting her life in danger?

And then Clint remembered what he had told Mickey.

"Mickey!" he shouted, but no sooner was the word out of his mouth he heard the shots.

Six of them.

EPILOGUE

Clint and Luke Short were ready to leave the next day. Clint didn't want to stay in Jericho Flats any longer than he had to.

They were walking their horses down Jericho's main street when Darlene came out of the saloon.

"Excuse me, Luke."

"Sure."

He dismounted and walked over to her, taking both her hands in his.

"What are you and the other girls going to do now?" he asked.

"We'll run the place ourselves. I mean, if it belongs to anyone it belongs to Mickey, but she's in no shape to make any decisions."

"I guess not. It's not every day that a girl kills her own father."

"We'll try and help her get through it. What about you, Clint?"

"What about me?"

"Will you ever come back this way?"

"Maybe," he said, but she saw "never" in his eyes and couldn't blame him.

She kissed him and said, "Be careful."

He nodded and started back to where Short was.

There was no one else in town he wanted to say good-bye to. Mickey had refused to see him, and he couldn't blame her. After all, it had been his instructions she'd been following when her father came through that door and she fired the New Line six times—incredibly hitting him all six times.

"Nice-looking lady," Luke said as Clint rejoined him.

"Yeah. What do you say we mount up?"

"Fine with me."

They did so and rode out of town.

"Tell me the truth," Luke said.

"About what?"

"You really figured out that I wasn't dead, that I had faked my death so I could come here in secret and help you?"

"Of course."

Clint didn't tell Luke that Sam Wing had given him a clue in his telegram.

"You did not. I'll bet you were as surprised as hell when I opened those livery stable doors."

"No, I wasn't."

"Was too."

"No. I expected you."

"Did not."

"Did too."

They rode on for a few moments and then Luke said, without looking at Clint, "Did not . . ."

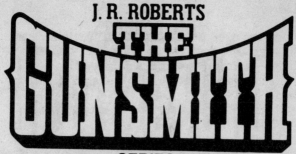

J. R. ROBERTS
THE GUNSMITH

SERIES

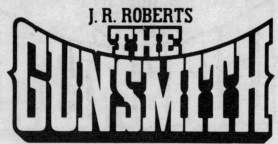

J. R. ROBERTS
THE GUNSMITH

SERIES